AF478125

Author Chronologies

General Editor: **Norman Page**, Emeritus Professor of Modern English Literature, University of Nottingham

Published titles include:

William Baker
A WILKIE COLLINS CHRONOLOGY

J. L. Bradley
A RUSKIN CHRONOLOGY

Michael G. Brennan and Noel J. Kinnamon
A SIDNEY CHRONOLOGY 1554–1654

Gordon Campbell
A MILTON CHRONOLOGY

Alison Chapman and Joanna Meacock
A ROSSETTI FAMILY CHRONOLOGY

Edward Chitham
A BRONTË FAMILY CHRONOLOGY

Martin Garrett
A BROWNING CHRONOLOGY
ELIZABETH BARRETT BROWNING AND ROBERT BROWNING
A MARY SHELLEY CHRONOLOGY

A. M. Gibbs
A BERNARD SHAW CHRONOLOGY

Graham Handley
AN ELIZABETH GASKELL CHRONOLOGY

J. R. Hammond
A ROBERT LOUIS STEVENSON CHRONOLOGY
AN EDGAR ALLAN POE CHRONOLOGY
AN H. G. WELLS CHRONOLOGY
A GEORGE ORWELL CHRONOLOGY

Edgar F. Harden
A WILLIAM MAKEPEACE THACKERAY CHRONOLOGY
A HENRY JAMES CHRONOLOGY
AN EDITH WHARTON CHRONOLOGY

Lisa Hopkins
A CHRISTOPHER MARLOWE CHRONOLOGY

John Kelly
A W. B. YEATS CHRONOLOGY

John McDermott
A HOPKINS CHRONOLOGY

Roger Norburn
A JAMES JOYCE CHRONOLOGY
A KATHERINE MANSFIELD CHRONOLOGY

Norman Page
AN EVELYN WAUGH CHRONOLOGY
AN OSCAR WILDE CHRONOLOGY

John Pilling
A SAMUEL BECKETT CHRONOLOGY

Peter Preston
A D. H. LAWRENCE CHRONOLOGY

Nicholas Maltzahn
AN ANDREW MARVELL CHRONOLOGY

Author Chronologies Series
Series Standing Order ISBN 0–333–71484–9
(*outside North America only*)

You can receive future titles in this series as they are published by placing a standing order. Please contact your bookseller or, in case of difficulty, write to us at the address below with your name and address, the title of the series and the ISBN quoted above.

Customer Services Department, Macmillan Distribution Ltd, Houndmills, Basingstoke, Hampshire RG21 6XS, England

A Katherine Mansfield Chronology

Roger Norburn

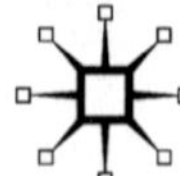

First published 2008 by
PALGRAVE MACMILLAN
Houndmills, Basingstoke, Hampshire RG21 6XS and
175 Fifth Avenue, New York, N. Y. 10010
Companies and representatives throughout the world

PALGRAVE MACMILLAN is the global academic imprint of the Palgrave Macmillan division of St. Martin's Press, LLC and of Palgrave Macmillan Ltd. Macmillan® is a registered trademark in the United States, United Kingdom and other countries. Palgrave is a registered trademark in the European Union and other countries.

ISBN-13: 978–0–230–52559–7   hardback
ISBN-10: 0–230–52559–8   hardback

This book is printed on paper suitable for recycling and made from fully managed and sustained forest sources. Logging, pulping and manufacturing processes are expected to conform to the environmental regulations of the country of origin.

A catalogue record for this book is available from the British Library.

A catalogue record for this book is available from the Library of Congress.

10   9   8   7   6   5   4   3   2   1
17   16   15   14   13   12   11   10   09   08

Printed and bound in Great Britain by
CPI Antony Rowe, Chippenham and Eastbourne

To Ruby and Elsa, two half-Kiwis

Contents

General Editor's Preface	viii
Acknowledgements	x
A Note on Names and List of Abbreviations	xii
Family Tree	xiv
Introduction	xvi
A Katherine Mansfield Chronology	1
Monetary Equivalents	92
A Who's Who in the Mansfield Chronology	93
Bibliography	130
Index	137

General Editor's Preface

Most biographies are ill-adapted to serve as works of reference – not surprisingly so, since the biographer is likely to regard his function as the devising of a continuous and readable narrative, with excursions into interpretation and speculation, rather than a bald recital of facts. There are times, however, when anyone reading for business or pleasure needs to check a point quickly or to obtain a rapid overview of part of an author's life or career; and at such moments turning over the pages of a biography can be a time-consuming and frustrating occupation. The present series of volumes aims at providing a means whereby the chronological facts of an author's life and career, rather than needing to be prised out of the narrative in which they are (if they appear at all) securely embedded, can be seen at a glance. Moreover, whereas biographies are often, and quite understandably, vague over matters of fact (since it makes for tediousness to be forever enumerating details of dates and places), a chronology can be precise whenever it is possible to be precise.

Thanks to the survival, sometimes in very large quantities, of letters, diaries, notebooks and other documents, as well as to thoroughly researched biographies and bibliographies, this material now exists in abundance for many major authors. In the case of, for example, Dickens, we can often ascertain what he was doing in each month and week, and almost on each day, of his prodigiously active working life; and the student of, say, *David Copperfield* is likely to find it fascinating as well as useful to know just when Dickens was at work on each part of that novel, what other literary enterprises he was engaged in at the same time, whom he was meeting, what places he was visiting, and what were the relevant circumstances of his personal and professional life. Such a chronology is not, of course, a substitute for a biography; but its arrangement, in combination with its index, makes it a much more convenient tool for this kind of purpose; and it may be acceptable as a from of 'alternative' biography, with its own distinctive advantages as well as its obvious limitations.

Since information relating to an author's early years is usually scanty and chronologically imprecise, the opening section of some volumes in this series groups together the years of childhood and adolescence. Thereafter each year, and usually each month, is dealt with separately. Information not readily assignable to a specific month or day is given as a general note under the relevant year or month. The first entry for each month carries an indication of the day of the week, so that when necessary this can be readily calculated for other dates. Each volume also contains a bibliography of the principal sources of information. In the chronology itself, the sources of many of the more specific items, including quotations, are identified in order that the reader who wishes to do so may consult the original contexts.

NORMAN PAGE

Acknowledgements

For permission to quote from the works of Katherine Mansfield I am greatly indebted to The Society of Authors as the Literary Representative of the Estate of Katherine Mansfield. I am also indebted to the Random House Group Ltd. for permission to quote from *The Letters of Virginia Woolf* edited by Nigel Nicolson and Joanne Troutmann and *The Diaries of Virginia Woolf* edited by Anne Olivier Bell, published by The Hogarth Press and to Harcourt, Inc. (*The Letters of Virginia Woolf Volume II: 1912–1922* edited by Nigel Nicolson, © by Quentin Bell and Angelica Garnett and *The Diary of Virginia Woolf, Volume I: 1915–1919*, © 1977 by Quentin Bell and Angelica Garnett and *Volume II: 1920–1924*, © 1978 by Quentin Bell and Angelica Garnett.)

Books such as these are invariably collaborative undertakings and I would also like to thank the following: my wife, Mary Norburn, who has whole-heartedly supported this project despite her continuing ill health; Andrew Gillott who compiled the table of monetary equivalents; Andrew Norburn who formatted the family tree once I had provided him with the details; Lee Shufflebotham who expertly surfed the net for me; Jonathan and Kate Norburn who did some research for me in New Zealand which included confronting Katherine Mansfield's diabolical handwriting. Claire Cook whose industry and skill as a typist I am constantly in awe of and Norman Page, the General Editor of the Author Chronologies Series, whose helpfulness and patience know no bounds.

It has been extremely useful to correspond, via e-mail, with Margaret Scott and Julie Kennedy. Margaret Scott has put every Mansfield reader, researcher and biographer in her debt not only for co-editing the *Collected Letters,* itself a major accomplishment, but also for the monumental achievement of transcribing Mansfield's more-than-fifty notebooks and scores of unbound papers into the two-volume *Katherine Mansfield Notebooks.* (My text frequently employs the phrase 'In her notebook…' as if they were one seamless whole, which of course they are not.) She helped me towards answers to many questions arising mostly from the letters and notebooks.

Julie Kennedy, whose great little book *Katherine Mansfield in Picton* contains the only Beauchamp family tree I have come across in extensive reading and research for the Chronology, explored several tricky problems of dating and interpretation with me. From the Katherine Mansfield Birthplace in Wellington I received a great deal of support and encouragement: thanks are especially due to its director, Mary Morris, and to Sheanagh Guilliard who effectively nailed the date (over which biographers and other commentators have disagreed) when Mansfield left Wellington Girls' High School and started to attend Miss Swainson's school. Margaret Connell, the Principal of Queen's College, Harley Street, London, clarified when the Easter term would have ended in 1906. Any merits the book has are owing to all these people. I alone am responsible for its faults.

Finally, I would like to thank the staff of Lincolnshire Libraries for their professionalism in dealing with my many requests for books and articles and also the staff at the Alexander Turnbull Library, Wellington, the British Library, London, and the Hallward Library of the University of Nottingham. Last of all, but certainly not least, I would like to thank the Author's Foundation of the Society of Authors without whose exceedingly generous grant I would not have been able to undertake this work.

A Note on Names and List of Abbreviations

When someone is first mentioned in the Chronology he/she is given a forename as well as a surname, e.g. Floryan Sobieniowski and Dorothy Brett. Thereafter the forename is dropped unless that would cause ambiguity. Thus Aldous Huxley remains Aldous Huxley as his brother Julian puts in an appearance, Vanessa Bell is always such as Clive Bell enters the narrative and so on. The aim is to prefer being over-explicit to being mysterious. Although Hardy is pretty obviously Thomas Hardy after his first appearance, the reader might struggle with Lewis or even James, hence Wyndham Lewis and Henry James. Katherine Mansfield's sisters, whether married or not, are always given their Beauchamp surname. 'Aunt Belle' (one of Mansfield's mother's sisters) emphasizes the family connection and hints at her chaperonage. The author of *Elizabeth and her German Garden* is referred to as Elizabeth Beauchamp throughout. This avoids the potential confusion of tracking her surname as it changes because of her marriages, but more positively emphasizes the family heritage, both writers, Katherine and Elizabeth, being descended from John Beauchamp, 'The Poet of Hornsey Lane'.

The names of some people occur so frequently in the Chronology that they are abbreviated after their first appearance:

KM (a shortened form she occasionally used herself) refers to Katherine Mansfield. I have retained the abbreviation for her in the 'Who's Who...' section.

Others:

AB	Annie Beauchamp, mother
DHL	David Herbert Lawrence
FL	Frieda Lawrence
HB	Harold Beauchamp, father
JMM	John Middleton Murry
LB	Leslie Beauchamp, brother
LM	Ida Baker (in books and articles, as in life, frequently referred to as L.M.)

OM   Ottoline Morrell
VW   Virginia Woolf

The following abbreviations are used for KM's books:

BOS   *Bliss and Other Stories*
DNOS   *The Doves' Nest and Other Stories*
GPOS   *The Garden Party and Other Stories*
IGP   *In a German Pension*
SCOS   *Something Childish and Other Stories*

In the Chronology KM is the subject of the verb where no subject is otherwise indicated.

Family Tree

Edward
Beauchamp
Born: c. 1750
Died: Unknown

Jane
Beauchamp

John
Beauchamp
Born: 1781
Died: c. 1850

Anne
Stone
Married: 1815

Henry Herron
Beauchamp
Born: 1825
Died: 1907

Elizabeth Weiss
Lassetter
Married: c. 1855

Horatio
Beauchamp
Born: 1826
Died: 1896

Annie Mary
Lassetter
Married: c. 1853

Charlotte
Beauchamp
Born: c. 1855
Died: Unknown

George
Waterlow

Sydney
Beauchamp
Born: 1861
Died: 1921

Mary Annette
Beauchamp
Born: 1866
Died: 1941

(1) Count Henning
von Arnim
Married: 1890

(2)
John, 2nd Earl Russell
Married: 1916

Connie
Beauchamp
Born: 1858

Sydney
Waterlow
Born: 1878
Died: 1944

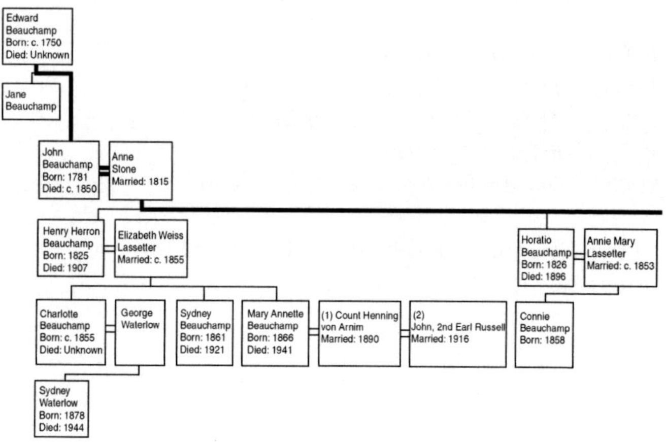

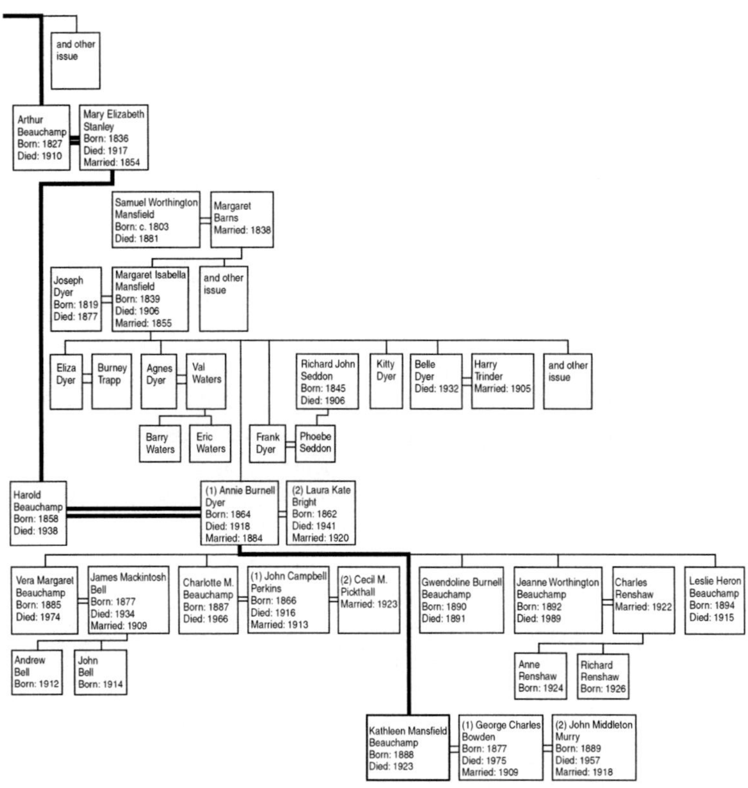

and other issue

Arthur Beauchamp
Born: 1827
Died: 1910

Mary Elizabeth Stanley
Born: 1836
Died: 1917
Married: 1854

Samuel Worthington Mansfield
Born: c. 1803
Died: 1881

Margaret Barns
Married: 1838

Joseph Dyer
Born: 1819
Died: 1877

Margaret Isabella Mansfield
Born: 1839
Died: 1906
Married: 1855

and other issue

Eliza Dyer

Burney Trapp

Agnes Dyer

Val Waters

Richard John Seddon
Born: 1845
Died: 1906

Kitty Dyer

Belle Dyer
Died: 1932

Harry Trinder
Married: 1905

and other issue

Barry Waters

Eric Waters

Frank Dyer

Phoebe Seddon

Harold Beauchamp
Born: 1858
Died: 1938

(1) Annie Burnell Dyer
Born: 1864
Died: 1918
Married: 1884

(2) Laura Kate Bright
Born: 1862
Died: 1941
Married: 1920

Vera Margaret Beauchamp
Born: 1885
Died: 1974

James Mackintosh Bell
Born: 1877
Died: 1934
Married: 1909

Charlotte M. Beauchamp
Born: 1887
Died: 1966

(1) John Campbell Perkins
Born: 1866
Died: 1916
Married: 1913

(2) Cecil M. Pickthall
Married: 1923

Gwendoline Burnell Beauchamp
Born: 1890
Died: 1891

Jeanne Worthington Beauchamp
Born: 1892
Died: 1989

Charles Renshaw
Married: 1922

Leslie Heron Beauchamp
Born: 1894
Died: 1915

Andrew Bell
Born: 1912

John Bell
Born: 1914

Anne Renshaw
Born: 1924

Richard Renshaw
Born: 1926

Kathleen Mansfield Beauchamp
Born: 1888
Died: 1923

(1) George Charles Bowden
Born: 1877
Died: 1975
Married: 1909

(2) John Middleton Murry
Born: 1889
Died: 1957
Married: 1918

Introduction

Katherine Mansfield died at the tragically early age of 34. In the course of her short professional life as a writer she produced 88 stories (89 if one includes 'The Aloe', the first version of 'Prelude'), some of them unfinished, many published only posthumously. During almost all of her adult life she suffered from ill health. Her last years are a record of her increasingly desperate attempts to find a cure for her tuberculosis and at the same time write, put down on paper, what was still in her head so that she did not leave, as she once said, only 'scraps'. This chronology attempts to trace her life first in outline from her birth in Wellington, New Zealand, in 1888 to the end of 1905, when she was in her second year at Queen's College, Harley Street, London, and then in more detail from 1906 to her death in Avon, near Fontainebleau, in 1923.

This task is not always easy. 'I am a secretive creature to my last bones' she writes to the faithful Ida Baker in March 1922. Although she carefully covered her tracks, much of her life has now been well documented mainly because Middleton Murry preserved so much. Gaps in the narrative remain, however, particularly in the period between her return to England in August 1908 and her meeting Murry at the end of 1911. It is likely that certain aspects of her life during the last months of 1908 and the first of 1909, in particular, will never be entirely clarified and however much biographers may regret this, and resort to speculation, the obscurity would surely be of immense satisfaction to Katherine Mansfield herself.

One of the ways of hiding one's identity, or confusing the issue, that commentators, biographers, chronologists must all be alert to is by name changes and the use of pseudonyms. This starts in childhood with her siblings. Thus her sister Charlotte Mary becomes Chaddie but is also Marie; her brother Leslie is Chummy but also Bogey – a name she uses for Murry as well. Kathleen Mansfield Beauchamp herself soon becomes Katherine Mansfield – but also Julian Mark, Karl Mansfield, Lili Heron, Elizabeth Stanley, Boris Petrovsky and some 20 other names used in her writing, in correspondence and with friends and acquaintances. Part and parcel of her shifting identities is her love of performance, of acting in plays – and then not always keeping to the script (Chronology, Christmas 1914) – her dressing up, her mimicry (she earned money both as a mimic and a film extra). The difficulty is to find the real Katherine Mansfield behind all those masks.

The opposite danger to becoming confused and lost in all the dressing up, play-acting and name changes is to be over-subtle in interpretation. For example, it is easy to see some coded message in the fact that she married George Bowden in March 1909 dressed entirely in black. Bowden himself made nothing of it as it was the one good costume she had at the time. Similarly, in her correspondence, it is easy to overstate the different personae she adopts in writing to different people – her father (whose annual allowance to her she wanted at all costs to maintain), her sisters, Middleton Murry (a huge range of emotions on display there, if not different personalities), Richard Murry, Ida Baker, Virginia Woolf, Garnet Trowell, Ottoline Morrell and others. We all write differently according to who our correspondent is, what we want to say, what we want to obtain from the correspondence.

The truth is that, in a great age of letter-writing, Katherine Mansfield, expansive, witty, insightful and, yes, honest, is an outstanding letter-writer. Like the *Notebooks,* the four volumes of the *Collected Letters* which have already appeared (the final volume, covering 1922, is still to be published) are enormously valuable to the chronologist. I have mined them not only for their intrinsic narrative information but also a) to flag up the miniature short stories they sometimes contain (e.g. her journey from Paris to Bandol in January 1918, told to four different correspondents, and her experience of German long-range shelling of Paris in March 1918), but more importantly b) to highlight letters in which she illuminatingly discusses her art, e.g. the letter to Dorothy Brett of 11 October 1917, the letters to Murry of 3 February 1918 and 10 November 1919 and the letter of 26 May 1921 to Marie Belloc-Lowndes. Mansfield was nothing if not serious about the art of writing and how it needed total re-thinking in the second and third decades of the twentieth century. For a few short years she was at the heart of the modernist movement. Reading her stories, letters and notebooks over 80 years after her death one is staggered at her modernity.

A Katherine Mansfield Chronology

(The names of individuals in the 'Who's Who…' are printed in **bold** on their first appearance in the Chronology.)

Early years (1888–1905)

1888   (Sunday, 14 October) Kathleen Mansfield Beauchamp (KM) is born at 8 a.m., the third child of **Harold Beauchamp** (HB), a merchant, and **Annie Burnell Beauchamp** (AB) (née Dyer) at 11 (now 25) Tinakori Road, Wellington, New Zealand. The other children are Vera Margaret (1885–1974), Charlotte Mary ('Chaddie') (1887–1966), Gwendoline Burnell (1890–1891), Jeanne Worthington (1892–1989) and **Leslie Heron** (LB) (1894–1915).

1889   (January) HB, aged 30, becomes a partner in the Wellington importing firm, W.M. Bannatyne and Company.

(c. April) At the age of six months is taken with her sisters to visit relatives on South Island.

(Tuesday, 6 August) **John Middleton Murry** (JMM) is born in Ethnard Road, Peckham, London.

(November) HB and AB make their first trip to England. The three children so far born are left in the capable hands of Granny Dyer (née Mansfield), AB's mother, and Aunt Belle (Isabel Dyer), a sister of AB's, both of whom live with the family.

1890   (Saturday, 11 October) Gwendoline Burnell Beauchamp is born.

1891   (Friday, 9 January) Gwen dies of infantile cholera. The following day she is photographed being held by Granny Dyer with a doll's house in the background.

1892   (Friday, 20 May) Jeanne Worthington Beauchamp is born.

1893   (Easter) The Beauchamps move to Chesney Wold, a 14-acre property in the country at Karori, a few miles outside Wellington. (KM's story 'Prelude' records this move.) The family begins to spend summers at Anakiwa, near Picton, on South Island.

1894   (Wednesday, 21 February) Leslie Heron Beauchamp (LB) is born. HB takes over an importing firm and makes Walter Nathan, a neighbour from Tinakori Road, a partner. (His family appears in 'Prelude' as the Samuel Josephs.)
   (December) Visits Picton with her family.

1895   (early in the year) Attends school for the first time, joining Vera and Chaddie Beauchamp at the Karori Public School to which all the local children go.
   HB becomes a member of the Wellington Harbour Board.

1897   Wins the school composition prize for an essay entitled 'A Sea Voyage'.

1898   HB and AB leave for England on a second visit. The children are again looked after by Granny Dyer and Aunt Belle.
   (Wednesday, 25 May) Enters Wellington Girls' High School, a bus ride away.
   (September) 'Enna Blake' appears in *The High School Reporter*, KM's first published story. *Elizabeth and her German Garden* by Elizabeth von Arnim (née Beauchamp) [henceforward referred to as **Elizabeth Beauchamp**], a first cousin of HB, is published to immediate acclaim.
   (November) On their return from England HB and AB move with their family back to Wellington, 75 Tinakori Road (the setting for 'The Garden Party').
   (Christmas) The Beauchamps take a holiday cottage at Island Bay, Wellington, on the Cook Strait, and are joined there by Marion Ruddick who met HB and AB as they were travelling back to New

Zealand and has become a friend of KM. HB becomes a director of the Bank of New Zealand and around this time buys (or rents) a cottage near Day's Bay on Wellington Harbour's eastern side.

1899 KM's story 'A Happy Christmas Eve', which anticipates 'The Doll's House', appears in *The High School Reporter*. KM also receives prizes for English, French and Arithmetic.

1900 (June) Begins to attend, with her elder sisters, Miss Swainson's private school at 20 Fitzherbert Terrace. There she starts keeping notebooks, writes poetry and founds a school magazine. Meets Maata Mahupuku (or Martha Grace), a wealthy Maori girl who is 18 months her junior.

1901 (Tuesday, 4 June) Begins 'Three 20th Century Girls'.
    (Sunday, 3 November) After attending a church service and hearing a sermon on the Maoris, records in her prayerbook her intention to become a Maori missionary.

1902 Becomes infatuated with **Thomas Trowell**, a brilliant young cellist who performs under the name of Arnold Trowell. A fund has been set up to enable him and his twin brother, **Garnet**, a violinist, to study in Europe. Inspired by 'Caesar' (as she calls him) KM begins to take cello lessons from his father.

1903 (Wednesday, 7 January) The *New Zealand Mail* notes the departure, due later in the month, of the Beauchamp family for England.
    (29 January) Leaves for England with HB, AB (who has just made her will and given a farewell tea party), her sisters, LB, Aunt Belle and an uncle.
    (end of January to mid-March) On board the cargo ship, *Niwaru*, the entire passenger accommodation of which her family occupies. The ship stops for a day at Las Palmas in the Canary Islands where a photograph is taken of the party with the ship's captain. KM writes to her friends, including Tom Trowell, and composes poetry.
    (Thursday, 16 April) From 27 St Stephen's Square, Bayswater, describes her excited reaction to London, Westminster Abbey, St Paul's, the British Museum, the Tate Gallery and Hampstead Heath.

(29 April) With Vera and Chaddie Beauchamp enters Queen's College, 45 (and 43) Harley Street, to finish her education. Immediately meets **Ida Baker** (LM) who is to become her life-long friend and companion, and quickly begins to idolize the professor of German, Walter Rippmann, who is to introduce her to the work of Oscar Wilde. KM boards next door at 41 Harley Street.

(August) The Beauchamps stay briefly at Brompton House, Malvern, from which KM writes to her cousin Sylvia Payne who, like her sister Evelyn, entered Queen's College before the Beauchamp girls. Writes stories and poems.

(Autumn) May pay a fleeting visit to the Trowell brothers who are now studying in Frankfurt. Meanwhile HB ad AB return to New Zealand with Jeanne and LB. Aunt Belle remains in London to chaperon her nieces.

(December) KM's story 'The Pine-Tree, the Sparrows, and You and I' appears in the *Queen's College Magazine*. Spends the Christmas holidays with Vera and Chaddie Beauchamp at the home of her great-uncle, Henry Herron Beauchamp (father of Elizabeth Beauchamp), in Bexley, Kent.

1904   (Saturday, 2 January) Travels with Chaddie Beauchamp to Wortley, near Sheffield, to stay with distant relatives.

(6 January) Tells Payne she longs to hear from her and see her. She will return to London on 12. Encloses a poem written on New Year's Eve, 'The Old Year and the New Year'.

(24 January) Describes to Payne her adoration of Rippmann but finds her fellow pupils very dull.

(March) KM's story 'Die Einsame' ('The Lonely One') appears in *Queen's College Magazine*.

(July) Lists books read, music studied, letters written and writing done. Amongst the books she has enjoyed are *Life and Letters of Byron* by Thomas Moore, *The Dolly Dialogues* and *Rupert of Hentzau* by Anthony Hope and *Poems* by E.A. Poe.

(Friday, 15 July) The Russian short story writer and dramatist, Anton Chekhov, dies of tuberculosis.

(Monday, 12 September) Inscribes to LM '*Two Songs: Love's Entreaty* and *Night,* words by Kathleen M. Beauchamp and music composed by Vera M. Beauchamp' and the following day inscribes them to Tom Trowell.

(October/November) Actively participates in debates of the Queen's College Debating Society, sometimes proposing or seconding motions.

(December) KM's story 'Your Birthday' appears in *Queen's College Magazine*.

(Monday, 26 December) Writes to Payne from Bexley expressing her friendship for her and her love of writing and small children.

1905   (Sunday, 1 January) Having just returned from a midnight service writes emotionally to Thomas Trowell.

(February) Has a minor operation on one of her feet in a nursing home in John Street, WC1. Her rendition on the cello of Tchaikovsky's 'Sérénade Melancholique' is appreciatively received at a school concert.

(July) KM's story 'One Day' appears in *Queen's College Magazine*.

(December) KM's story 'About Pat' (i.e. Patrick Sheehan, the Beauchamps' cowman-gardener at Karori) appears in the *Queen's College Magazine* which she co-edits for this issue. For the third successive year spends Christmas with her elder sisters at the Bexley home of Henry Herron Beauchamp and his wife Louise.

1906

EVENTS, THE ARTS, LITERATURE: Liberals win a landslide victory in the British General Election (Feb.); Suffragettes gain in strength and support; Dreyfus completely vindicated in France (July); deaths of Ibsen (May) and Cézanne (Oct.); John Galsworthy publishes *The Man of Property*; Rudyard Kipling, *Puck of Pook's Hill*; Jack London, *White Fang*; E. Nesbit, *The Railway Children*; Upton Sinclair, *The Jungle*; Bernard Shaw's *The Doctor's Dilemma* staged.

January
1 (Mon)   Sees in the New Year at Eastbourne, Sussex.

March
2 (Fri)   Writes two short poems 'What, think you, causes me truest Joy' and 'The Students' Room'.
16   Inscribes to LM a copy of Poe's *Tales of Mystery and Imagination*.

April
During the Easter vacation is taken with her sisters by Aunt Belle first to Paris then to Brussels where KM meets the Trowell twins who are students at the Conservatorium.

13 (Fri)   HB and AB arrive in England for a six-month stay before taking their daughters back to New Zealand.

15   Easter Day

20   The Beauchamp family are now all staying at Fripps Hotel, 30 Manchester Street, London.

24   Writes to Payne from Fripps Hotel, telling her that HB is opposed to her becoming a professional cellist so she will devote herself to writing in which she can impersonate others, a satisfying activity. Believes strongly that women should be able to lead their own lives independent of men.

May
18 (Fri)   Begins what is now known as *Juliet,* her first attempt at sustained fiction. (It will be abandoned early in 1907 when KM is back in Wellington.)

June
2 (Sat)   May attend a dramatic recital given by Blanche Theeman at the Aeolian Hall.

July
14 (Sat)   Leaves Queen's College at the end of the Easter term as do Vera and Chaddie Beauchamp. Is given a thick note-book by Clara Wood 'In very affectionate remembrance of 41 Harley Street'.

22   Stays with AB at her great-uncle, Henry Herron Beauchamp's house.

August
31 (Fri)   Writes to her cousin Lulu Dyer from 43 Harley Street.

September
22 (Sat)   Writes the macabre story 'Les deux étrangères'.

October
1 (Mon)   Writes the prose fragment 'Quelque chose' beginning 'I walk along the broad almost deserted street…'

| 14 | KM's 18th birthday. She is staying with her great-uncle Henry Herron Beauchamp. |
| 18 | The Beauchamp family sets sail from Gravesend for New Zealand on the S.S. *Corinthic*. (Only Aunt Belle, who has married a ship owner, W. Harry Trinder, remains in England.) |

November

During the sea voyage, via Capetown, develops a short-lived passion for a member of the England cricket team who are going to tour New Zealand. KM's notebooks also reveal her extreme dissatisfaction with her parents and the prospect of returning to her native land.

December

| 6 (Thurs) | The Beauchamps arrive back in Wellington. |
| 31 | Granny Dyer, who has left 75 Tinakori Road to live with another daughter, dies suddenly before KM has a chance to visit her. |

1907

EVENTS, THE ARTS, LITERATURE: Boy scouts go camping for the first time (July); New Zealand becomes a Dominion within the British Empire (Sept.); Marconi initiates a transatlantic wireless service from Nova Scotia to Ireland (Oct.); *Lusitania* breaks all records for crossing the Atlantic (Oct.); Kipling wins Nobel Prize for Literature (Dec.); deaths of Grieg (Sept.) and Francis Thompson (Nov.); Picasso's 'Les Demoiselles d'Avignon' exhibited (March); Puccini's *Madame Butterfly* first performed in English in London (Aug.); Joseph Conrad publishes *The Secret Agent*; Edmund Gosse, *Father and Son*; E.M. Forster, *The Longest Journey*; J.M. Synge's *The Playboy of the Western World* staged in London.

January

| 8 (Tues) | Tells Payne she feels friendless and desolate and longs to be back in London. The death of her grandmother has horrified her. |
| 21 | Writes the prose poem 'L'Incendie', signing it 'Karl Mansfield'. |

February
Spends time at Island Bay, wishing LM were with her.

March
Around this time AB holds a garden party at 75 Tinakori Road. The day is spoilt by a fatal accident to a young man living in a nearby cottage. These events will form the basis for KM's story 'The Garden Party'.

April

10 (Wed) On her 17th birthday Mahupuku receives a letter from KM praising her beauty. In her notebook at about the same time KM makes clear her physical desire for Mahupuku.

13 The *Freelance* notes that HB has been 'elected chairman of the Board of the Bank of New Zealand'. Soon after the family moves to a bigger, grander house in Thorndon, 47 Fitzherbert Terrace.

May

5 (Sun) Writes 'Vignette – Through the Autumn afternoon' (originally simply entitled 'Vignette').

June

1 (Sat) Spends at least the first days of the month in a small cottage at Day's Bay where she experiences a lesbian relationship with Edith Bendall.

25 Finds her book of child verses (for which Bendall has done some illustrations) absurd. She hates everyone, including herself, except for Thomas Trowell.

29 By now is admitting that she and Bendall bore each other. She wants Mahupuku.

July

22 (Mon) Tells Martha Putnam (HB's current secretary who is typing her work for her) that she prefers to write pessimistic poems.

August

11 (Sun) Writes passionately to Thomas Trowell. (However it is unlikely that the letter is posted as the opening lines will

be copied very closely in her letter of 13 October 1908 to Garnet.)

20   Confides her longing to be with Thomas to her note-book.

27   Rapturously enjoys her cello playing with Mr Trowell, thinking of Thomas all the time.

28   Receives a letter from LM about Thomas that leaves her feeling depressed, isolated and angry.

September

Mr and Mrs Trowell leave New Zealand to join their sons in England. In her notebook KM urges herself to be strong, to stand up against HB and convince him that she must make the same journey.

23 (Mon)   Tells E.J. Brady, the editor of the *Native Companion*, a Melbourne periodical, that the 'Vignettes' which she has submitted to him are very much her own work and that she hates plagiarism. (Brady has felt that they resembled Wilde's work too much.) She goes on to give some details about herself.

October

1 (Tues)   The *Native Companion* publishes 'Vignettes' for which KM receives £2*.

5   Writes the poem 'London is calling me'.

10   Unbeknown to her, HB thanks Brady for encouraging his daughter and confirms her age and originality.

11   Thanks Brady herself for his encouragement and the cheque and informs him that she wants to be read only as 'K. Mansfield' or 'KM'.

14   KM's 19th birthday. Her family holds a dance for her.

21   Complains bitterly about her family in her notebook and longs for London and, on 22 or 23, declares that she is in love only with herself.

November

1 (Fri)   The *Native Companion* publishes KM's 'Silhouettes'.

9   Drafts the 'Vignette – Summer in Winter'.

c.16   At the start of a month-long camping trip in North Island leaves Wellington by train with Millie Parker, a music friend, for Hastings, arriving at her destination in the evening and staying with Parker's relations, the Ebbetts.

17   The four are joined by four others (Mr Hill, Mr and Mrs Webber and Ann Leithead) and set off in two wagons each drawn by two horses. They camp that night in Eskdale, north of Napier.

18   Begins drafting a letter to Chaddie Beauchamp en route for Te Pohue where the party camps for the night.

19   To Tarawera.

20   Near the Waipunga Falls drafts a long, descriptive letter to AB. From there to Rangitaiki. (Years later KM will make use of the countryside between the Waipunga River and Rangitaiki for her story 'The Woman at the Store'.) Writes the poem 'In the Rangitaiki Valley' about now.

21   Heading north-east the party camps on the Kaingaroa Plains.

22   To the Troutbeck station near the township of Galatea.

23   South to Te Whaiti in the Urewera country.

24   Through spectacular scenery to Umuroa where the party camps.

25   After visiting Ruatahuna the party returns to the camp site at Te Whaiti. KM plays with Maori children and meets 'real English people', declaring in her notebook 'Give me the Maori and the tourist but nothing between'.

26   More contact with Maoris, the warmth of whose welcome will be reflected in KM's story 'How Pearl Button was Kidnapped'. The party travels north-west to Waiotapu the sulphur fumes of which make her sick.

27   The party reaches Rotorua, the northernmost point of the tour, staying there until 1 December. KM dislikes Rotorua even more than Waiotapu and is sick and miserable the whole time despite receiving family letters at the local branch of the Bank of New Zealand.

30   Meets Tom Seddon, son of the late Prime Minister, who has escorted her in Wellington. He takes her to lunch.

December

1 (Sun)   The party begins to travel south, reaching Atiamuri. KM starts to feel better and her mood lightens.

2	To Waikato Riverside camp. The *Native Companion* publishes 'In a Café' and 'In the Botanical Gardens', the latter signed 'Julian Mark'. KM receives £2 7s 6d for them.
3	The party explores the Huka Falls before reaching Lake Taupo, camping in the grounds of the Terraces Hotel and staying there about a week during which time KM writes a vignette 'Sunset Tuesday'.
11	After lunch at Rangitaiki the party travels over the Rununga plain to camp beside a roadman's cottage. KM mentally collects more material which she will use in her story 'The Woman at the Store'.
12	The party probably camps at Tarawera again.
13	The party probably camps at Te Pohue again.
14	Final campsite in Eskdale.
15	Arrives back in Hastings and writes a poem 'Youth', an image of which anticipates the opening of Section VI of 'At the Bay'.
16	Visits Napier, meeting Bendall there.
17	Returns to Wellington by train.

Towards the end of 1907 sends apologetically – because of its apparent lesbian content – her story 'Leves Amores' (='Casual Loves') to Putnam for typing.

1908

EVENTS, THE ARTS, LITERATURE: Proposal for Old Age Pensions in Britain is passed (June); the Model T Ford goes on sale (Oct.); the Suffragette leaders Emmeline and Christabel Pankhurst are jailed (Oct.); Rutherford wins the Chemistry Nobel Prize for his work on the nature of the atom and radioactivity (Dec.); opening of exhibition of Van Gogh paintings in Paris (Jan.); Arnold Bennett publishes *The Old Wives' Tale*; Forster, *A Room with a View*; Kenneth Grahame, *The Wind in the* Willows; H.G. Wells, *The War in the Air*.

January

17 (Fri)	In a chatty letter to Vera Beauchamp (who is in Sydney) mentions a sketch she has just written, 'The Education of Audrey', and a concert of Tom Trowell's in London which has been very well received.

23   Whilst waiting for a concert which Clara Butt is giving
                   in Wellington drafts a letter in German to Tom Trowell
                   telling him she will leave for England in March.

February
Drafts the 'Vignette – By the Sea'.
10 (Mon)   Records in her notebook 'I shall end of course – by
                   killing myself'.

March
4 (Wed)   Writing from Day's Bay, where she is staying with
                   Chaddie Beauchamp, tells Payne that she hopes to leave
                   for London in April. She cannot live with HB. She has
                   finished her first book. (KM may be referring to her book
                   of child verses on which Bendall collaborated.)
18   The *Dominion* (Wellington) announces that Miss Kathleen
                   Beauchamp is leaving in April for London. (This does
                   not materialize.)

April
Writes 'The Thoughtful Child. Her Literary Aspirations' dedicated to
Bendall.
12 (Sun)   Attends the Polo Ball with Chaddie Beauchamp.

May
Responds positively to Elizabeth Robins's novel *Come and Find Me*.
Summarizes her needs as 'power, wealth and freedom'.
8 (Fri)   Enrols at Wellington Technical School for 'Commercial
                   Subjects' (typing and book-keeping).
17   Agitatedly tells herself that her destiny lies in her own
                   hands.

June
'The Tiredness of Rosabel' dates from this month. (It will be published posthumously in *Something Childish and Other Stories* (SCOS,
1924).)
6 (Sat)   'The Lonesome Child', a poem, appears in the *Dominion*
                   signed 'Kathleen Beauchamp'.
19   Attends a tea party at which violets are the theme,
                   winning first prize for her four-line poem on violets.

Writes to Vera Beauchamp that she is leaving in July taking only her notebooks and photographs.

27   KM's violet poem 'Why Love is Blind' is published in the *New Zealand Free Lance*.

July

1 (Wed)   'Study: The Death of a Rose' (a prose poem) is published in the *Triad* (Dunedin). Attends a farewell party, reported in the local press, hosted in her honour by Eileen Ward, the daughter of the Prime Minister, Sir Joseph Ward.

6   Having sailed with HB and AB from Wellington to Lyttleton, South Island, a few days before, leaves New Zealand alone on the *Papanui*. The ship in its seven-week journey calls at Montevideo and Tenerife.

August

24 (Mon)   After disembarking at Plymouth, arrives by train in London to be met by LM with whom she stays for some days at Montagu Mansions near Baker Street. KM then moves to Beauchamp Lodge, Warwick Crescent, Paddington, a hostel for unmarried women (mainly music students). There meets Margaret Wishart. Her allowance from HB is £100* a year.

September

Transfers her affections from Tom to Garnet Trowell to whom she writes a series of passionate love letters during the next few months whilst he is touring with the Moody-Manners Opera Company, herself frequently staying at the Trowell family home at 52 Carlton Hill, St John's Wood.

9 (Wed)   Probably attends a concert of nineteenth century music at Queen's Hall.

13   Sees Garnet off to Birmingham at the start of the opera company's winter season.

17   Goes to report on a Suffrage Meeting in Baker Street.

22   Writes 'October', a poem dedicated to Vera Beauchamp (subsequently the title will be altered to 'November').

Autumn: obtains professional invitations from hostesses to use her talents for mimicry and recitation at social gatherings. This helps KM financially.

October

1 (Thurs)	Writes the short prose piece 'Youth and Age'.
3	Attends a recital by the Venezuelan pianist Teresa Carreño at the Bechstein Hall, meeting her backstage afterwards.
14	KM's 20th birthday. Receives a ring from Garnet Trowell through the post. After visiting Carlton Hill, goes to stay at Melrose, Upper Warlingham, Surrey, a property owned by Harry Trinder, the husband of her Aunt Belle.
19	Returns to Beauchamp Lodge.
20	With Wishart leaves for Paris, travelling via Newhaven–Dieppe and arriving early on 21 at the Gare St. Lazare. Whilst in Paris attends the wedding of a naval friend of the Wisharts. (Wishart's father is an admiral).
23	Visits Versailles.
25	Does the reverse journey back to London, arriving at Beauchamp Lodge in the evening.
29	Visits a Mrs Charley Boyd who puts her mind at rest (KM has feared pregnancy after an adventure in Montevideo en route for England). Writes four short poems which she immediately sends to Garnet.

November

2 (Mon)	Sends Garnet Trowell the words for two songs composed by Tom Trowell (one is 'A Song for Summer', the other has not survived) and her poem 'The Winter Fire'.
4	Reveals to Garnet her ambitious plans for the art of elocution and public recitation of her own work.
5	Writes affectionately to Vera and Jeanne Beauchamp.
7	Attends, as a guest of Wishart's family, the launching of the battleship HMS *Collingwood* staying briefly at 44 Keyham Terrace, HM Dockyard, Devonport.

December

4 (Fri)	Writes the poem 'Revelation'.
9	Writes the poem 'The Trio'.
11	Writes the 'Vignette – I look out through the window'.

KM's life during the last few weeks of 1908 and the first few of 1909 are extremely obscure. There are few incontrovertible facts. She stays for some weeks at Carlton Hill but finally falls out with Mr and

Mrs Trowell and returns, probably in January 1909, to Beauchamp Lodge. At some point, either November–December 1908 or March 1909, becomes pregnant by Garnet Trowell.

1909

EVENTS, THE ARTS, LITERATURE: Selfridge's opens in London (March); Peary reaches the North Pole (April); Bleriot flies across the English Channel (July); deaths of Synge (March), Algernon Swinburne (April) and George Meredith (May); Diaghilev's Ballets Russes perform for the first time (May); André Gide publishes *La Porte étroite*; Thomas Hardy, *Time's Laughingstocks and Other Verses*; Ezra Pound, *Personae* and *Exultations*; Gertrude Stein, *Three Lives*; Wells, *Ann Veronica* and *Tono-Bungay*.
Writes a story 'His Sister's Keeper' this year.

January
30 (Sat)   'The Education of Audrey' appears in the *Evening Post* (Wellington).

February
Meets **George Bowden** at the home of Dr C.W. Saleeby in Hamilton Terrace, St John's Wood.

March
2 (Tues)   Marries Bowden at Paddington Registry Office. LM is the only witness. After some hours together leaves him and returns to Beauchamp Lodge.
3   Leaves Beauchamp Lodge and spends a week alone in London, probably in a flat in the Paddington area.
c.10   Joins Garnet Trowell now on tour with the Moody-Manners Opera Company in Glasgow and then accompanies them all to Liverpool.
17   The *Morning Post* announces her marriage to Bowden.
Late this month returns to London, staying with LM.

April
Early this month moves to a flat in Maida Vale.
8 (Thurs)   Having heard of KM's marriage, AB leaves for England.

14   The *Weekly Graphic* (New Zealand) announces KM's sur-
            prise marriage.
Late this month travels to Brussels declaring in her notebook
that she must escape England which she loathes. Nevertheless, on
29 leaves for London again.

May

27 (Thurs) AB arrives, installing KM in the Manchester Street hotel
            and subsequently interviewing both Bowden and LM's
            father.
Late this month is taken by AB to the continent.
31   From the Hotel Marquardt, Stuttgart, writes an account
            of the journey through Holland and Germany.

June

Records her struggle to avoid taking veronal to obtain a good night's
sleep.
4 (Fri)   Arrives with AB at the spa town of Bad Wörishofen,
            some 50 miles west of Munich. They check in at the
            Hotel Kreuzer, Kneippstrasse.
10   Having returned to London, AB sails for New Zealand.
12   Moves to Pension Müller, Türkheimerstrasse. (This becomes
            the setting for the stories of KM's first published book
            In a German Pension (*IGP*, 1911).)
Late this month (?) miscarries.

Summer, or early Autumn, meets the Pole **Floryan Sobieniowski**
and, some time after meeting him, writes what is now one of her
best-known poems 'To Stanislaw Wyspiansky'.

July

Late this month AB reaches Hobart, Tasmania, where she is met
by HB. During the voyage a fellow passenger, previously unknown
to her, has died in her arms. These events form the basis for KM's
story 'The Stranger'.

August

1 (Sun)   (or 31 July) Moves to stay with Fräulein Rosa Nitsch,
            the owner of a lending library above the post office on

Kasinoweg. (It may be around this time that, as a result of her request to LM, a young boy from a London slum named Charlie Walter is sent to live with her until the autumn.)

13   Arriving back in Wellington, AB cuts KM out of her will.

September

23 (Thurs) Moves to Kaufbeurerstrasse 9, staying with the Brechenmacher family whose name KM will make use of in *IGP*.

October

1 (Fri)   KM's 1907 child's verse 'A Day in Bed' is published in the *Lone Hand* (Sydney) signed 'K. M. Beauchamp'.
14   KM's 21st birthday.

November

3 (Wed)   KM's poem 'November' (originally 'October') is published in the *Daily News* (London).
10   Sends Christmas greetings to Jeanne Beauchamp and tells her she has bought a Polish dictionary with the money she sent her for her birthday.

December

12 (Sun) At a time when KM and Sobieniowski (who is currently in Warsaw) are exchanging love letters, Vera French, a London friend, writes to KM pleading with her not to live with him.
21   LM writes making arrangements for KM's return to England and sending her money for the fare. KM does return, probably shortly after Christmas, and stays at the Strand Palace Hotel, London.

1910

EVENTS, THE ARTS, LITERATURE: Edward VII dies and is succeeded by George V (May); the Girl Guides movement is founded (May); Dr Crippen is arrested, caught by radio on a ship off Canada (July); Edison demonstrates talking motion pictures (August); deaths of

Mark Twain (April), Henri 'Douanier' Rousseau (Sept.), Holman Hunt (Sept.) and Tolstoy (Nov.); publication of the 'Futurist Manifesto' of painting in Milan (Jan.); Stravinsky's *Firebird* is performed by the Ballets Russes (June); Bennett publishes *Clayhanger*; **Walter De la Mare**, *The Return*; Forster, *Howards End*; Wells, *The History of Mr Polly*.

January
Approaches Bowden and suggests that they live together. He agrees and KM moves into his flat at 62 Gloucester Place, Marylebone, either late this month or early February.

February
At Bowden's suggestion takes 'The Child-Who-Was-Tired' to **A.R. Orage**, the editor of the *New Age*. KM's poem 'The Pillar-Box' appears in the *Pall Mall Magazine*.
24 (Thurs) 'The Child-Who-Was-Tired' appears in the *New Age*. Orage asks KM for more stories.

March
KM's story 'Mary' is published in the *Idler*.
3 (Thurs)   'Germans at Meat' appears in the *New Age*.
10   'The Baron' appears in the *New Age*.
24   'The Luft Bad' appears in the *New Age*.
Late this month has an operation during which her left fallopian tube is removed as it is affected with gonococci. (This operation has serious implications for her health for the rest of her life.) At KM's insistence LM takes her from the nursing home and installs her first of all in her Marylebone flat.

April
LM takes KM to some rooms above a shop in Rottingdean, on the Sussex coast, where she is visited by Bowden, convalesces for the next few months and writes the poems 'The Sea Child', 'The Opal Dream Cave' and 'Sea'. During her stay suffers from what she believes to be rheumatism but in fact originates from gonorrhoea.
28 (Thurs) HB's father, Arthur, dies in Picton.

May
26 (Thurs) 'Loneliness', a sonnet written whilst KM was staying with Bowden earlier in the year, appears in the *New Age*.

July

7 (Thurs)	'At Lehmann's' appears in the *New Age*.
21	'Frau Brechenmacher Attends a Wedding' appears in the *New Age*.
29	LM, writing on KM's behalf, returns the ring Garnet Trowell had given her, telling him she is now 'Katherine Mansfield' (i.e. not only in print) and living at 39 Abingdon Mansions, Pater Street, Kensington. This is the home of Orage and **Beatrice Hastings**.

August

4 (Thurs)	'The Sister of the Baroness' appears in the *New Age*.
11	In a letter entitled 'A Paper Chase' in the *New Age* deplores press and police behaviour in the Crippen murder case.
18	'Frau Fischer' appears in the *New Age*.
25	In a letter entitled 'North American Chiefs' in the *New Age* deals ironically with literary life in North America.

Late summer, rents a flat from the painter Henry Bishop at 131 Cheyne Walk, Chelsea, overlooking the Thames. Meets **William Orton** (their relationship will be carefully described by him in his 1937 novel *The Last Romantic*) and may have an affair with Francis Heinemann.

October

14 (Fri)	KM's 22nd birthday.

December

'A Fairy Story' signed by 'Katherine Mansfield' (sic) appears in the *Open Window*.

26 (Mon)	Sobieniowski's translation (free in parts) of KM's poem 'To Stanislaw Wyspiansky' appears in *Gazeta Poniedzialkowa* (Cracow).

1911

EVENTS, THE ARTS, LITERATURE: The Sidney Street siege in London (Jan.); Copyright Act extends copyright to 50 years after an author's death (April); £1.5m made available to local authorities to build sanatoria for the eradication of consumption (May); Amundsen is first to the South Pole (Dec.); Marie Curie wins Chemistry Nobel

Prize for her work on the radioactive elements polonium and radium (Dec.); deaths of Mahler (May) and W.S. Gilbert (May); première of Richard Strauss's *Der Rosenkavalier* in Dresden; G.K. Chesterton publishes *The Innocence of Father Brown*; Conrad, *Under Western Eyes*; **D.H. Lawrence** (DHL), *The White Peacock*; Wells, *The New Machiavelli*; Edith Wharton, *Ethan Frome*.

January
On Bishop's return from Morocco moves to a flat at 69 Clovelly Mansions, Grays Inn Road.

April
It has been speculated that about this time KM is again pregnant and has the pregnancy terminated. There is very little, if any, documentary evidence for this. Furthermore, the operation of March 1910 may have rendered conception impossible for her. LM is summoned to join her father in Rhodesia.

May
During the month the Beauchamps arrive in London to attend the coronation of King George V and are re-united with KM.
18 (Thurs) 'A Birthday' appears in the *New Age*.
20   By now KM has arrived with Hastings at Ditchling-on-Sea, Sussex.
25   'A.P.S.A.' (='A Pleasant Sunday Afternoon') appears in the *New Age* signed 'KM and BH'. It takes the form of a letter parodying several contemporary authors including Chesterton, Alfred Austin, Bennett and Wells.

June
22 (Thurs) 'The Modern Soul' appears in the *New Age*. The coronation of George V takes place.
29   'The Festival of the Coronation (with apologies to Theocritus)' appears in the *New Age*.

Summer, JMM founds the quarterly magazine *Rhythm* with **Michael Sadleir** and becomes its editor.

July
KM is seriously ill with pleurisy (it is now regarded as an early sign of her tuberculosis).

August

To convalesce KM travels first to Bruges, then to Geneva where she stays at a Mme. Bieler's house, 8 rue Saint-Léger. LM, having returned from Rhodesia to London, joins her there.

17 (Thurs) 'The Breidenbach Family in England' appears in the *New Age*. (This is unsigned and of doubtful authenticity.)

24 'The Journey to Bruges' appears in the *New Age*.

September

Returns to London, spending much time with her family and renewing her friendship with Orton.

6 (Wed) Writes an account of her violent love-making of yesterday with a man whom she does not identify. Writes a short poem 'The world is beautiful tonight'.

7 'Being a Truthful Adventure' appears in the *New Age*. (When this story is published in *SCOS* the first word of the title will be omitted.)

October

5 (Thurs) 'Along the Gray's Inn Road' appears in the *New Age*. This is a prose poem about a man and his piano-organ, but it is made to look ridiculous by being printed as a letter to the editor.

11 Writes to J. B. Pinker, a literary agent, asking to see him before sending him her work.

14 KM's 23rd birthday.

19 'Love Cycle', verse parodies of Katherine Tynan, Nesbit, Wilfrid Gibson and Laurence Housman, appears in the *New Age*.

November

2 (Thurs) 'The Making of Gwendolen' by 'Mouche' appears in the *New Age*. (KM's authorship of this story is disputed.)

December

Early this month, *IGP*, 13 stories, ten of which have appeared in the *New Age*, is published by Charles Granville under the name of 'Stephen Swift'. During the month it will be reviewed in the *Athenaeum*, *Manchester Guardian*, *Daily Telegraph*, *New Age* (probably by Hastings), *Morning Post* and *Spectator*.

Late this month, meets JMM at the home of W.L. George, 84 Hamilton Terrace, St John's Wood. (JMM has been excited by KM's story 'The Woman at the Store' which she has sent him for *Rhythm*.)

1912

EVENTS, THE ARTS, LITERATURE: The *Titanic* sinks in the Atlantic (April); Air mail service opens between Paris and London (August); Edward Carson, leader of the Ulster loyalists, pledges to fight Irish Home Rule (Sept.); death of Strindberg (May); première of ballet *L 'Après Midi d'un Faune* based on Claude Debussy's tone poem (May); E.C. Bentley publishes *Trent's Last Case*; De la Mare, *The Listeners and Other Poems*; DHL, *The Trespasser*; Saki (i.e. H.H. Munro), *The Unbearable Bassington*; Shaw, *Pygmalion*.

January

27 (Sat)   JMM, writing from Oxford, tells KM about Victor Neuberg, whose book of poetry he has asked her to review, and his plans for *Rhythm*.

February

Spends time in Geneva, again staying at 8 rue Saint-Léger. By the end of the month KM is staying with Hastings and Orage near Crawley in Sussex.

March

7 (Thurs)   'A Marriage of Passion' and 'At the Club' appear in the *New Age*.

8   The Beauchamp family leaves England for New Zealand. KM will not see AB again.

28   A *New Age* review (probably by Hastings) viciously attacks the Spring issue of *Rhythm*, which has just appeared, singling out for special venom KM's story 'The Woman at the Store' and her poems (which she has claimed to be translated from the Russian of 'Boris Petrovsky') 'Very Early Spring' and 'The Awakening River'.

Late this month, JMM, now staying with his parents at 13 Nicosia Road, Wandsworth Common, writes several times to KM, briefly commenting on the *New Age* attack.

April

11 (Thurs) At KM's invitation JMM moves into a room at 69 Clovelly Mansions. Some weeks later they become lovers.

12 Leaves a note for JMM: 'This is your egg. You must boil it. K.M.'

18 The *New Age* returns to the attack on *Rhythm* in an article (probably by Orage) savaging in particular KM's work.

May

During the month, travels with JMM to Paris for a 'honeymoon'. There meets **Francis Carco**, *Rhythm's* Paris correspondent, and the painter **J.D. Fergusson**.

2 (Thurs) Orage, under the pseudonym of R.H. Congreve, launches a weekly series of attacks on KM ('Marcia Foisacre') until 6 June.

23 Writes to Bowden in response to his idea that they obtain an American divorce. Nothing comes of this idea as it is discovered that such a decree would be invalid in England.

June

'The Sea Child', a poem written at Rottingdean, 'The Meaning of Rhythm' (with JMM) and a brief, dismissive review of Galsworthy's *Moods, Songs and Doggerels* appear in *Rhythm* which from now on will be mostly under the imprint of Stephen Swift who pays JMM and KM (now assistant editor) £10* a month.

13 (Thurs) 'Puzzle: Find the Book', a pastiche, appears in the *New Age*. Mid-month, accompanies JMM to Oxford and stays with him at Boars Hill while he takes his final examinations. Around this time KM meets JMM's parents at their home. The visit is not a success and leads to estrangement between JMM and his family.

Summer, meets Frank Harris, **Edward Marsh** and **Henri Gaudier-Brzeska**.

July

Reviews *The Triumph of Pan* by Neuberg and (briefly) *The Green Fields* by Kenneth Hare for *Rhythm* in which her and JMM's article 'Seriousness in Art' also appears.

4 (Thurs)   'Green Goggles', a parody of Russian writers, appears in the *New Age*.

August
'Tales of a Courtyard' appears in *Rhythm* as does KM's review of *Elsie Lindtner* by Karin Michaelis and her and JMM's 'Jack and Jill attend the theatre'. (The latter is a review in dialogue form of Synge's *The Well of the Saints*. It is signed 'The Two Tigers', a sobriquet KM and JMM have recently acquired.)

September
The poem 'The Earth-Child in the Grass' signed 'Boris Petrovsky' appears in *Rhythm* as do the story 'How Pearl Button was Kidnapped' signed 'Lili Heron', 'Spring in a Dream' and KM's review of August Strindberg's *Confession of a Fool*.

4 (Wed)   Moves with JMM to Runcton Cottage, Runcton, near Chichester, Sussex. Soon Rupert Brooke and Marsh come to stay for a weekend. Sobieniowski, discovering their address, begins to sponge on them.

21   Reviews **Frank Swinnerton**'s *The Happy Family* in the *Westminster Gazette*.

End of the month (or beginning of October), Granville absconds, leaving JMM and KM with serious financial difficulties. Marsh, Brooke, Swinnerton, Wells and **Gilbert Cannan** are amongst those who will help to keep *Rhythm* in business and Martin Secker undertakes to publish the magazine from November.

October
The stories 'New Dresses' and 'The Little Girl', the former with a woodcut by Gaudier-Brzeska and the latter signed 'Lili Heron', appear in *Rhythm*, as do 'Sunday Lunch' (signed 'The Tiger') and KM's review of *An Anthology of Modern Bohemian Poetry* edited by P. Selver.

5 (Sat)   Tom Mills, who in 1907 had recommended that KM send her 'Vignettes' to the *Native Companion*, reviews *IGP* in the *Feilding Star* (New Zealand).

14   KM's 24th birthday.

November
Because of their financial difficulties KM and JMM have to move to a one-room flat in Chancery Lane, Holborn, and then to a slightly

larger flat at 57 Chancery Lane which, however, doubles as an office. KM's poem 'To God the Father' appears in *Rhythm* 'Translated from Boris Petrovsky'. Gaudier-Brzeska, having allegedly overheard KM criticizing his partner Sophie at Runcton, breaks with her and JMM.

28 (Thurs) KM's story 'The House' appears in Harris's magazine *Hearth and Home*.

December

'The Opal Dream Cave' and 'Sea', poems written at Rottingdean, appear in *Rhythm*.

25 (Wed) Spends Christmas with JMM, the Cannans and **Gordon** and **Beatrice Campbell** in Paris where they are entertained by the artist Anne Estelle Rice whose paintings momentarily overwhelm her. (Rice will marry the journalist and art critic O. Raymond Drey in 1913. See the 'Who's Who...' under **Anne Estelle Drey**.)

27 'Old Cockatoo Curl', written by KM and JMM, appears in the 'Christmas Number' of *T. P.'s Weekly*.

1913

EVENTS, THE ARTS, LITERATURE: The Suffragette Emily Davison dies after throwing herself in front of the king's horse at the Derby (June); the Panama Canal opens (Oct.); Stravinsky's ballet *The Rite of Spring* causes uproar at its Paris première (May); Robert Bridges becomes the new Poet Laureate (July); Alain-Fournier publishes *Le Grand Meaulnes*; Robert Frost, *A Boy's Will*; DHL, *Sons and Lovers*; Thomas Mann, *Der Tod in Venedig*; Marcel Proust, Vol. I of *A la recherche du temps perdu*.

KM acts as an extra in a few film productions.

January

The story 'Ole Underwood' and the poem 'Jangling Memory', signed 'Boris Petrovsky', appear in *Rhythm* as does 'Virginia's Journal' signed 'Virginia' which is, however, of doubtful attribution.

2 (Thurs) The *New Age* contains abusive attacks on KM and JMM written by Hastings.

8 The official opening of the Poetry Bookshop. Marsh describes the event to KM and JMM in the evening and spends more time with them later in the month.

18	The poem 'Floryan nachdenklich' appears in the *Saturday Westminster Gazette*.
26	In response to KM's request for a story, DHL, who is in Italy, suggests that 'The Soiled Rose' be published simultaneously in *Rhythm* and *Forum* and asks her to contact Edward Garnett, who is acting as his literary adviser, for the text.
30	Writes to Garnett agreeing to DHL's suggestion.

February

Early in the month, tells Garnett she explained to DHL that *Rhythm* does not pay. (DHL himself has accepted this.)

March

3 (Mon)	'Floryan nachdenklich' is reprinted in the *Dominion* (Wellington).
15	The poems 'There Was a Child Once' signed 'Boris Petrovsky' and 'Sea Song' appear in *Rhythm*. (This is the last issue of the magazine.)

Spring: at the suggestion of the Cannans, who own a converted windmill nearby, moves to 'The Gables', a cottage in Cholesbury, Buckinghamshire. JMM joins her at weekends. Sobieniowski also turns up.

May

KM's story 'Pension Séguin', first of the 'Epilogue' series, appears in the first issue of the *Blue Review* (successor to *Rhythm*) as does DHL'S story 'The Soiled Rose' (which he later reworks and renames 'The Shades of Spring').

Early this month, describes her night fears to JMM.

12 (Mon)	Gaudier-Brzeska and George Banks (a woman artist who has also contributed to *Rhythm*) attack JMM in his office in Chancery Lane, demanding payments for drawings published in *Rhythm* and the return of any of their work he still holds.
13	Discusses problems concerning Sobieniowski, Gaudier-Brzeksa and Banks in a letter to JMM.
19	Insists to JMM that she absolutely cannot cut 'Epilogue II' (posthumously known as 'Violet') for the June *Blue Review*. She means every word of it, as if writing with acid.

Late in this month (or June), explains to JMM that she hates having time-consumingly to act the housewife when she has creative work to do.

June
During this month, with JMM meets DHL and Frieda Weekley (later **Frieda Lawrence**) when they visit Chancery Lane. KM's stories, 'Millie' and 'Epilogue II' appear in the *Blue Review*.

July
KM's story 'Bains Turcs', the third in the 'Epilogue' series, appears in the last issue of the *Blue Review*. Acts as a go-between for Weekley and her son Montague.

1 (Tues)	Moves with JMM to 8 Chaucer Mansions, Queen's Club Gardens, West Kensington.
19	Reviews *Lu of the Ranges* by Eleanor Mordaunt in the *Saturday Westminster Gazette*.
26	Accompanies JMM and Gordon Campbell to Kingsgate, Broadstairs, Kent, where they stay with DHL and Weekley for the weekend. Returning on 28 on the train reads, and is deeply impressed by, *Sons and Lovers* which DHL has given her and JMM.

August

2 (Sat)	Completes drafting a chapter-by-chapter plan of a novel to be called *Maata*.
13	Completes the first chapter of *Maata*.

During the summer/early autumn accompanies JMM to Howth, near Dublin, to stay with the Campbells.

October

11 (Sat)	Describes various ailments she has had to Jeanne Beauchamp. She is looking forward to her birthday, which is always important to her, and has written a story 'Old Tar', which is set in the Karori countryside.
14	KM's 25th birthday.
25	'Old Tar' appears in both the *Westminster Gazette* and the *Saturday Westminster Gazette*.

November

16 (Sun)   Completes the second chapter of *Maata* but writes no
            more of the novel.
c. 27   DHL writes lengthily to JMM about the latter's relation-
            ship with KM. (This follows one from JMM to him partly
            on the same subject.)

December

Moves with JMM to Paris during the month. (JMM is to review
French books for the *Times Literary Supplement*.) (*TLS*.) **Frederick
Goodyear** accompanies them.

11 (Thurs) The *New Zealand Times* reprints 'Old Tar' with the sub-
            title 'A Karori Story'.
22   Writes to Chaddie Beauchamp from Hotel de l'Univers,
            9 Rue Gay-Lussac, telling her they have found a flat at
            31 Rue de Tournon to which they will move after Christ-
            mas. She is looking forward to life in Paris.

1914

EVENTS, THE ARTS, LITERATURE: Irish Home Rule Bill receives
its first Commons reading (April); Archduke Franz Ferdinand is
assassinated in Sarajevo (June) causing widespread disturbance
throughout Europe and leading eventually to the outbreak of world
war in August; battles of Mons and Tannenberg (Aug.); stalemate on
the western front by November; death of Alain-Fournier (in action)
(Sept.); Frost publishes *North of Boston*; Hardy, *Satires of Circum-
stance*; James Joyce, *Dubliners*; DHL *The Prussian Officer*; W.B. Yeats,
Responsibilities.
JMM dates KM's poems 'Countrywomen' and 'Stars' this year.

January

Early this year, writes 'Something Childish But Very Natural', her
longest story to date (published in *SCOS*).

17 (Sat)   Begins to keep careful weekly records of her expenditure
            in Paris.

February

 7 (Sat)   Reads Theocritus for much of the day.

10	Back in England JMM is well received at the Bankruptcy Court but he must file a statement of his business affairs at once. Having done this he returns to Paris on 13.
24	Leaves 31 Rue de Tournon with JMM to return to London. They take a furnished flat at 119 Beaufort Mansions, Chelsea, which JMM had told KM about on 6. The rent is £2 2s. a week.
28	Makes a careful record of money in hand and expenditure (and on 1 March).

March

6 (Fri)	Beginning a new notebook, records a disturbing dream she has just had.
19	Dreams delightfully about New Zealand.
20	Has a more painful dream about New Zealand.
23	Feels that LM is oppressive. She was happy in Paris mainly because LM was not there.
24	Thinks of AB on her birthday. She would love to see her again but does not think she will.
25	Spends an enjoyable day with LM during which they visit some of their old haunts.
26	Takes a tram to Clapham with LM.
27	LM leaves for Rhodesia where she will remain for two years. KM writes a poem about their parting called 'The Meeting'. JMM takes his public examination at Oxford.

April

During the month KM and JMM move to less expensive but miserable rooms at 102 Edith Grove, off Fulham Road. They both quickly succumb to pleurisy.

1 (Wed)	In her notebook criticizes JMM for his lack of empathy.
3	Would like to live on a barge with JMM (as her husband) and a son.
4	Very lonely. She is dissatisfied with her writing.
5	Records her realization of her profound love for JMM.
6	Feels LM is slipping from her mind.

May
Spends time with JMM at Pulborough, Sussex, during the month. About this time JMM receives the offer of a post in the Imperial Library at St Petersburg which he declines.

July
KM and JMM move to a flat at 111 Arthur Street, Chelsea, which they quickly discover is infested by bugs.

13 (Mon)   Attends with JMM the wedding of DHL and Frieda Weekley (henceforward FL) at Kensington Register Office, Marloes Road. FL gives KM her former wedding ring which she wears for the rest of her life and takes to her grave.

August

5 (Wed)   Following the outbreak of war the previous day, JMM enlists in a cyclists' battalion but, having second thoughts, quickly obtains medical exemption.

17   Records that she now regards Turgenev as a poseur and hypocrite.

24   KM and JMM put on paper their resolution to go and live by the sea in Devon or Cornwall as soon as they can rid themselves of current commitments.

30   Records her lack of trust in JMM, but also their decision to leave for Cornwall the next day.

September
Probably writes the poem 'Deaf House Agent' this month.

c.16 (Wed)   KM and JMM, after holidaying in Cornwall, move to a cottage at Udimore, near Rye, Sussex.

21   Writes to Laura Kate Bright, a Wellington friend of AB's, about London in wartime.

25   Returns to 111 Arthur Street, Chelsea.

October

c.11 (Sun)   KM and JMM travel to Chesham, Buckinghamshire, where they stay with DHL and FL who help them prepare the cottage which they are to move into three miles away.

14   KM's 26th birthday.

26   KM and JMM move to Rose Tree Cottage, The Lee, near
                Great Missenden and begin to experience the quarrels
                between DHL and FL.

November

6 (Fri)   The *Evening Post* (Wellington) publishes an unacknow-
                ledged excerpt from KM's letter of 21 September to Bright
                beginning 'Here in London, we are in the throes of this
                frightful war...'
9   JMM makes a will leaving everything to KM.
15   Having just reread Colette's *L'Entrave*, expresses her deep
                admiration for the French writer.
16   JMM receives a letter from Carco which KM comments
                on in her notebook. She feels close to him. (Subsequently
                he writes directly to her expressing his love for her.)

December

By now KM, dissatisfied with JMM, is conducting a passionate
correspondence with Carco.

15 (Tues)   Emotionally thanks HB for his Christmas gift of five
                sovereigns.
23   KM and JMM attend a Christmas party at DHL and FL's
                cottage. Also present are the Cannans, **S.S. Koteliansky**,
                Gordon Campbell and **Mark Gertler**.
25   A second Christmas party is held at the Cannans' with
                the same people present. In a playlet devised by JMM,
                KM departs from the script when, after making passion-
                ate love to Gertler (who, unbeknown to him, represents
                Carco), she refuses to be reconciled to JMM.

1915

EVENTS, THE ARTS, LITERATURE: Second battle of Ypres begins
in which the Germans use gas for the first time (April); the liner
Lusitania is torpedoed (May); Zeppelin air raids on the east coast
of the U.K. (June); the Gallipoli campaign fails (Dec.); Einstein's
General Theory of Relativity; death of Brooke (April) whose *1914
and Other Poems* is published posthumously; Ford Madox Ford
publishes *The Good Soldier*; DHL, *The Rainbow*; Somerset Maugham,
Of Human Bondage; **Virginia Woolf** (VW), *The Voyage Out*.

January

6 (Wed)   Records her longing for Carco in her notebook, but dare not push her thoughts 'as far as they will go'.

9   Is visited by DHL and Koteliansky who make plans to which KM is deeply opposed.

10   KM and JMM visit DHL leaving FL, who has just had a row with the latter, at Rose Tree Cottage.

12   Completes 'Brave Love' but is puzzled by it. (The story will not be published until March 1972.)

14   Receives a letter from Carco inviting her to stay with him in Gray. (Gray, near Dijon, is not near the Front, but is in the War Zone.)

16   Feels enormously encouraged by Campbell in her work after she reads 'Brave Love' to him.

17   Records that hatred of England possesses her this day.

23   Following a letter and photograph from Carco, feels passionately in love with him.

26   Attends a Marie Lloyd performance after travelling to London and being put up at Drey's.

29   Still in London meets Koteliansky who brings her a skirt, cigarettes and chocolates.

31   Having returned to Rose Tree Cottage, confides in her notebook that JMM understands that she wants to live in London apart from him.

February

3 (Wed)   LB arrives in England for military training.

4   Finishes Dostoevsky's *Crime and Punishment* which she thinks is very bad.

6   Receives another, urgent invitation from Carco.

8   Travels to London. It is probably during the next few days that, through DHL, she meets **Ottoline Morrell** (OM) for the first time. This meeting is at the latter's house in Bloomsbury.

c.10   Bumps into LB at the Bank of New Zealand. He, doubtless briefed by KM, reports back to their family on 11 that she loves JMM more than ever and their literary prospects are quite good. He may also give her money which in fact finances her visit to Gray.

16	Arrives in Paris.

16   Arrives in Paris.

19   Arrives at Gray where she meets Carco. (This whole episode is dramatized in her story, 'An Indiscreet Journey', dated by JMM 1915, but not published until it appears in *SCOS*.)

25   Returns to England and Rose Tree Cottage.

26   In letters to Koteliansky complains of severe rheumatism and, a little over a week later, 'mysterious pains' which have made her take to her bed.

March

Early in the month, sends 'The Little Governess' to Koteliansky for inclusion in the *Smart Set*. However, the story does not appear there.

13 (Sat)   With Koteliansky goes to stay the weekend with DHL and FL at Greatham, Pulborough, Sussex.

18   Returns to Paris to write, spending the first two nights in a hotel before moving to Carco's flat near Notre-Dame, 13 quai aux Fleurs, which he has placed at her disposal during his absence.

22   Attends a party at Hastings's flat and has a violent row with her after dancing with 'a very lovely young woman'. Later experiences an air raid on Paris which she describes to JMM.

24   Begins writing 'The Aloe' (which will eventually become 'Prelude') and has developed a liking for the work of Stendhal. JMM tells her that he has accidentally met Sobieniowski and given him his new address (95 Elgin Crescent, Notting Hill Gate).

26   Carco, writing under his disguise of 'Marguerite Bombard', invites KM to Gray again. She does not go.

27   By now is completely reconciled to JMM.

28   Tells JMM that she will not send any more work to Orage. (In fact she does.)

31   Returns to England to live with JMM in a flat at 95 Elgin Crescent.

May

5 (Wed)   Once more goes to 13 quai aux Fleurs to write. 'Spring Pictures' and 'An Indiscreet Journey' are probably written around this time. Meanwhile she is still working on 'The Aloe'.

c.7	Tells JMM that although she is writing mornings and afternoons she would like a real home with babies in it.
10	Is furious to discover that the other inhabitants of 13 quai aux Fleurs regard her as Carco's mistress.
14	Again affected by rheumatism of which she is sick and tired. Her work, however, she tells JMM, requires only polishing now.
15	Believes, she writes to JMM, that where the mob is concerned, there is no moral difference between any nation on earth, including England and Germany.
19	Returns to London, 95 Elgin Crescent.

June

KM and JMM move to 5 Acacia Road, St John's Wood, their first attractive home.

5 (Sat)	Gaudier-Brzeska is killed at the battle of Neuville St Vaast.

July

KM is introduced to **Bertrand Russell** by DHL.

August

25 (Wed)	Having just spent a week staying with KM and JMM whilst on a bombing instructors' course, LB writes home complimenting their house and the relationship between them.

September

11 (Sat)	JMM and DHL issue a leaflet about their new fortnightly journal the *Signature* which will include 'satirical sketches by Matilda Berry' (i.e. KM).
22	LB, having continued to visit KM at Acacia Road, leaves for France.

October

4 (Mon)	Under the name of Matilda Berry publishes 'Autumns: I' and 'Autumns: II' in the first issue of the *Signature*. (These stories are known later as 'The Apple-Tree' and 'The Wind Blows' respectively.)

7	LB is killed by a hand-grenade which explodes prematurely, whilst he is demonstrating how to throw them, at Ploegsteert Wood, near Armentières.
11	Is stunned and devastated when she hears the news of LB's death.
14	KM's 27th birthday.
18	Publishes the first part of 'The Little Governess' in the *Signature*, No. 2 as Matilda Berry.
29	Musing about LB's death, records in her notebook 'I welcome the idea of death…I long to join him' and later 'Then why don't I commit suicide? Because I feel I have a duty to perform to the lovely time when we were both alive. I want to write about it and he wanted me to…'.

November

1 (Mon)	Publishes the second part of 'The Little Governess' in the *Signature*, No. 3 as Matilda Berry. (This is the last *Signature* to appear.)
4	'Stay-laces', a dialogue, appears in the *New Age*.
5	Attends with JMM a party at **Dorothy Brett's** studio at which she meets her and other members of the Bloomsbury group, such as **Lytton Strachey**, for the first time.
11	Signs a tenancy agreement concerning 5 Acacia Road. (Koteliansky has part of the house and lives at that address for the rest of his life.)

Mid-month, leaves with JMM for the South of France.

19	Tells Koteliansky from Marseilles that she has heard that LB's last words were 'Lift my head Katy, I can't breathe'.
c.21	KM and JMM leave Marseilles for Hotel Firano, Cassis.
28	Prefers Cassis to Marseilles.

December

c.5 (Sun)	KM and JMM move to the Hotel Beau Rivage, Bandol.
7	JMM leaves for London. KM begins to keep a careful record of expenditure in her notebook.
9	Writing to JMM, gives her reasons for regarding *The Oxford Book of English Verse* (1900) 'a mass of falsity' and the French equivalent (1907) even worse.

12	Lists the symptoms of their 'Marseilles fever' to JMM, dysentery, shivering fits and loss of appetite.
13	Puts the fact that she cannot walk at all now down to her rheumatism.
14	Describes to JMM a shy but helpful Englishman who prescribes some ointment for her rheumatism. (This is **F. Newland-Pedley** whose kindness to KM continues until he leaves Bandol just after Christmas. Moreover the treatment works, as she tells JMM on Christmas Day.)
15	Is desperate for news from JMM and extremely hurt that he has not written.
19	Asks JMM to send her some Dickens and will respond to his request for something for the *Signature* which, he has told her, cannot do without her.
20	Feels better and is starting to love the South of France. DHL writes from Hampstead telling her that he and FL are soon going to move to Cornwall where he would like KM and JMM to join them, a request he is to repeat.
21	Is writing 'Et in Arcadia Ego' for the *Signature*.
22	Wants JMM to share her growing love of the countryside and people around Bandol. He tells her her loneliness and illness have shaken him.
24	Completes 'Et in Arcadia Ego'. Feels well and happy.
29	Enthusiastically describes to JMM the villa (Villa Pauline) which she has found for them and expresses her utter love for him.
30	JMM leaves for France.

31 (or 1 January) JMM arrives at the Villa Pauline, Bandol.

1916

EVENTS, THE ARTS, LITERATURE: Battle of Verdun begins (Feb.); Easter Rebellion in Dublin (April); battle of Jutland (May); battle of the Somme begins (July); Lloyd George becomes British Prime Minister (Dec.); deaths of Henry James (Feb.) and London (Nov.); Joyce publishes *A Portrait of the Artist as a Young Man*; DHL, *Amores* and *Twilight in Italy*; George Moore, *The Brook Kerith*; Pound, *Lustra*.

January

At the Villa Pauline during the next few weeks drafts several poems including, in all probability, her elegy 'To L.H.B. (1894–1915)'. Reads Shakespeare with JMM. They make a note of lines which particularly strike them.

22 (Sat) Records in her notebook 'Yes I want to write about my own country until I simply exhaust my store...it is a "sacred debt" that I pay to my country because my brother and I were born there...I want for one moment to make our undiscovered country leap into the eyes of the old world...Then I want to write poetry. I feel always trembling on the brink of poetry...But especially I want to write a kind of long elegy to you [LB] – perhaps not in poetry. No, perhaps in Prose – almost certainly in a kind of special *prose*.'

February

Goodyear, now a corporal in the Royal Engineers serving in France, is writing to KM.

13 (Sun) Confides in her notebook that she has written very little so far.

March

6 (Mon) Thanks HB profusely for raising her allowance from £10 to £13 a month (£156* p.a.). Is pessimistic about the war, mentioning Verdun to him.

8 DHL, now writing from Zennor, Cornwall, urges KM and JMM to come and live in an unoccupied house very close to him and FL.

12 Begins the notebook which brings 'The Aloe' to its conclusion.

16 AB notes that since LB's death KM has been writing loving letters to all the members of her family.

21 Travels to Marseilles staying at Hotel Oasis where she and JMM had briefly stayed the previous November.

c.23 Having met Chaddie Beauchamp, who has sailed from Bombay, returns to Bandol.

27 With JMM leaves Bandol to return to England.

April

4 (Tues)   Arrives with JMM in Cornwall for the reunion with DHL and FL, staying first at the Tinner's Arms, Zennor, whilst the four of them renovate their cottage at Higher Tregerthen.

c.17   KM and JMM move into their cottage near DHL and FL.

May

4 (Thurs)   Tells Beatrice Campbell she cannot believe she has written 'The Aloe' on re-reading it and is having second thoughts about living close to DHL because of his views and the violence of his life with FL.

11   Writes wittily and fully to Koteliansky about DHL's rages. Moreover she feels she does not belong in this stony countryside.

17   DHL and FL's violent life together is described in a letter to OM. KM and JMM are disgusted by them.

June

Mid-month, moves with JMM to Sunnyside Cottage, Mylor, on the south coast of Cornwall, 30 miles from Zennor. Their rent is £18 p.a.

24 (Sat)   Reveals to Koteliansky that the experience of Higher Tregerthen has deeply disturbed her.

27   Writing to OM, invites herself to Garsington for what will be her first visit.

July

Early this month, Goodyear visits KM and JMM at Mylor.

7 (Fri)   DHL, writing to Koteliansky, notes the strained relations between KM and JMM. He prefers the former.

8   Travels alone to London, staying with the Campbells at 24 Norfolk Road, St John's Wood.

13   Travels to Garsington, becoming better acquainted with several of the Bloomsbury group who are also there.

17   Returns to Sunnyside Cottage, Mylor.

20   Gertler complains to Koteliansky that, having arranged to see KM at Garsington, she had left before he arrived.

Late this month, DHL stays a few days with KM and JMM at Mylor.

August

15 (Tues) JMM travels to London in connection with obtaining a war job.

19 Finds Mylor intolerable without JMM and tells him the following day she cannot stay beyond October like this. Asks him to send her money.

22 Sends a good luck telegram to JMM for his interview at M.I.7.

25 Travels to London.

26 Joins JMM at Garsington for the weekend, then moves temporarily to Brett's studio at 4 Logan Place, Earls Court, London.

30 Publicly defends DHL's book of poems *Amores* when it is derided by other diners at the Café Royal. (This incident is used by DHL as 'Gudrun in the Pompadour', Chapter 28 of *Women in Love*.)

September

KM and JMM are now estranged from DHL, FL and Koteliansky.

4 (Mon) JMM begins work as a translator for the War Office at Watergate House, Adelphi.

6 Is currently at Garsington before returning again to Logan Place.

18 Makes arrangements with Mary Hutchinson to stay at her and St John Hutchinson's house at West Wittering, Sussex next weekend.

Late this month, moves with JMM to Maynard Keynes's house at 3 Gower Street, Bloomsbury. Brett and **Dora Carrington** also have flats in the house.

30 Is visited at Gower Street by Strachey who has tea with her.

Autumn, LM returns from Rhodesia. KM finds lodgings for her in Hampstead.

October

14 (Sat) KM's 28th birthday.

November

About this time meets VW for the first time.

23 (Thurs)   Dines with Russell. Keeps up a correspondence with him over the next few weeks.

December

3 (Sun)   Visits Garsington for a few days.

25   Spends Christmas at Garsington. Amongst those present, besides JMM, are Strachey, Brett, Carrington, Russell, **Aldous Huxley** and Maria Nys (who will marry Huxley in July 1919).

26   Hurriedly devises a playlet, 'The Laurels', in which she acts with JMM, Strachey, Carrington, Aldous Huxley and Nys.

1917

EVENTS, THE ARTS, LITERATURE: U.S. enters the war (April); third battle of Ypres begins (July); Bolshevik coup in Russia (Nov.) leads to Russian withdrawal from the war; deaths of Edward Thomas (in action) (April), Degas (Sept.) and Rodin (Nov.); J.M. Barrie's *Dear Brutus* is staged; Conrad publishes *The Shadow Line*; Eliot, *Prufrock and Other Observations*; DHL, *Look! We Have Come Through*; Siegfried Sassoon, *The Old Huntsman*; Yeats, *The Wild Swans at Coole*.

January

1 (Mon)   Writes part of the fragmentary 'Geneva' (which is later called by JMM 'Travelling Alone' and then, with other fragments, 'The Lost Battle').

2   Hopes OM will be able to persuade DHL not to publish *Women in Love*. She is searching hard for a studio. About this time also writes to JMM discussing the horrors of flat-hunting and speculating about their options for the future. They both must write in the year ahead.

12   With JMM dines with the Woolfs and **Sydney Waterlow** (KM's second cousin).

14   Informs OM that she thinks she has found a flat in Grays Inn for which she asks her to be a referee. Returns to the subject of DHL, saying he should be laughed at. She has had an 'appalling cold'.

16   Tells Russell that St John Hutchinson has refused her a reference [on the grounds of her living with JMM] and

	mentions her work as a film extra as she does in a letter to him of 21.
22	Apologizes to Russell for cancelling their appointment for 23 but her cough is vile and she does not want to inflict it on anyone else.
24	Agrees to dine with Russell on 26.

February

1 (Thurs)	Leaves 3 Gower Street and moves to 141A Old Church Street, Chelsea. Later this month JMM takes rooms at 47 Redcliffe Road, near KM's address, at a rent of £35* p.a.
6	Gives OM her new address.
11	VW tells her sister, Vanessa Bell, that she has had some sort of 'rapprochement' with KM but finds her 'unpleasant' and 'unscrupulous'.
c.13	Assures OM of her love and understanding of her.
24	Writes to Russell partly about his article 'The World After the War' which she likes except for the shocking last sentence. She is now reclusive, doing nothing but reading and writing. She will let him have 'Geneva' once it is finished. (This letter appears to conclude their relationship.)

March

The Woolfs set up their hand press at Hogarth House, Richmond.

c.16 (Fri)	Goodyear, now a second lieutenant, leaves for France.

April

3 (Thurs)	Rejects OM's invitation to Garsington for Easter as she is working very hard. She has a play half completed and has written stories, notes and sketches. But she is cold and sometimes frightened.
19	Publishes six 'Fragments' in the *New Age*: 'Alors, je pars', 'Living Alone', 'E.M. Forster', 'Beware of the Rain!', '"LM's" Way' and 'Cephalus'. She is critical of Forster's *Howards End*. He 'never gets any further than warming the teapot...but there ain't going to be no tea...'

At some point between now and June LM moves in with KM.

24	Mentions to OM the play 'A Ship in the Harbour' which she is still writing. (KM also refers to it as 'Toots' by

which name the unfinished work is published in 1971.)
She longs for the war to end.

26   VW tells Vanessa Bell she is going to approach KM for a
story for their new printing press. (During the summer
she will frequently visit KM at Old Church Street.)

May

3 (Thurs)   'Two Tuppenny Ones, Please', a dialogue, is published in
the *New Age* (reprinted in *SCOS*).

10   'Late at Night' is published in the *New Age* (reprinted in
SCOS).

17   'The Black Cap', a dialogue, is published in the *New Age*
(reprinted in *SCOS*).

19   Visits JMM's flat after he has left for a weekend at
Garsington. She writes that she left her own flat in terror
and declares her undying love for him.

22   Tells OM how hard she is working, relaxing only by going
to the Queen's Hall for concerts. She is re-reading Walt
Whitman.

23   Goodyear dies of wounds near Arras.

24   'In Confidence' is published in the *New Age*.

31   'The Common Round', a dialogue, presumably drawing
on KM's experiences as a film extra, is published in the
New Age. It will be incorporated in 'The Picture' published
in *Art and Letters*, Autumn 1919, which in turn will become
'Pictures' in *Bliss and Other Stories (BOS, 1920)*.

June

3 (Sun)   At Garsington with JMM. Reads the title poem of Eliot's
Prufrock and Other Observations, which is published this
month, to those present.

7   'A Pic-Nic' a dialogue (actually a film script), is published
in the *New Age*.

11   At JMM's flat meets Sassoon. (JMM helps him prepare his
public protest against the war.)

14   'Mr Reginald Peacock's Day' is published in the *New Age*
(reprinted in *BOS*).

16   Arranges to meet OM soon so that she can tell her about
her dinner with Julian and Aldous Huxley and Eliot. The
war oppresses her.

c.24	Describes to OM a dinner party at Mary Hutchinson's home. Among the guests were Robert Ross, Roger Fry, Eliot and Robert Graves whom KM grew to dislike. Tells, VW she feels that they are kindred spirits.
26	Dines at Hogarth House with VW who, although she finds her odd, reports positively on her reactions to KM in a letter to Vanessa Bell the following day.

July

3 (Tues)	Describes to OM the dinner with VW and recent visits by JMM and Aldous Huxley.
13	Attempts to express her complicated feelings about New Zealand to OM.
21–23	At Garsington with JMM who stays on after KM's return to London. Also there is JMM's younger brother, Arthur (i.e. **Richard Murry**).
26	VW tells Vanessa Bell that she and her husband have promised to publish KM's story. (This is 'The Aloe' which KM is refashioning as 'Prelude'.)

Late this month, criticizes JMM's article on the French writer Léon Bloy in a letter to him.

29	Dines with the Woolfs at Hogarth House.
30	Declines OM's offer of a cottage on the Garsington estate.
31	KM's doctor hints that English winters are extremely bad for her rheumatism.

August

10 (Fri)	Comments to JMM on individual poems of his which he hopes to include in a collection.
11	Although JMM has told her that OM fell deeply in love with him during his last stay at Garsington, reassures OM of her friendship despite her agony during recent weeks.
15	Describes to OM her reactions to the garden at Garsington (which is also the subject of her contemporary poem 'Night Scented Stock').

Mid-month, informs VW that the typist has 'Prelude'. She longs to travel to Asheham as she is suffering from rheumatism, depression and 'fury'.

18	Travels by train to Asheham, near Lewes, Sussex, to stay with VW, arriving late in the day. During her stay VW shows her 'Kew Gardens', a short story probably influenced by KM.
22	Leaves Asheham to return to Chelsea where she is visited by Fergusson with whom she feels a real rapport.
c.23	Reveals her excitement to VW that the two of them are pursuing very similar literary ends and praises her 'Kew Gardens'. Tells her that a painter friend wants to do some woodcuts for 'Prelude' (which she has delivered to the Woolfs).

September

6 (Thurs)	'M. Séguin's Goat' (a translation by KM from the French of Alphonse Daudet) is published in the *New Age*.
9	JMM writes to Richard Murry at Garsington about the farmhouse KM and they will find and develop after the war.
20	'An Album Leaf' is published in the *New Age* (reprinted, revised, as 'Feuille d'Album' in *BOS*).

October

4 (Thurs)	'A Dill Pickle' is published in the *New Age* (reprinted, revised, in *BOS*).
9	The Woolfs begin printing 'Prelude'.
10	Dines with the Woolfs at Hogarth House.
11	Attempts to describe to Brett her identification in her writing with what she is contemplating and her devotion to her art. In her diary VW records her trenchant opinions of KM but also praises her.
14	KM's 29th birthday.
17	Bowden v. Bowden is heard in London. The decree nisi will become absolute at the end of April 1918, freeing KM to marry JMM.

November

13 (Tues)	Having received the necessary paper, the Woolfs begin printing 'Prelude' in earnest.
19	Tells Brett that JMM has had a breakdown and must go where there is sunshine.

20	Informs OM that JMM is ill from depression and over-work and asks if she will put him up at her cottage in the grounds of Garsington. OM responds by telegram on 21 inviting them both to come at once.
21	Asks Brett, who will arrive at Garsington before JMM, to look after him there. His illness terrifies her.
24	JMM travels to Garsington. HB's mother, Mary Elizabeth Beauchamp (née Stanley), dies at Picton.

December

1 (Sat)	Travels to Garsington to be with JMM. During the journey in a dog cart from the station to the manor catches a chill which develops after her return to London (probably on 3) into a serious lung condition.
6	German bombs drop on London, something KM alludes to in a letter to Brett the following day.
7	Tells OM that her bad cough and general feeling of ill health will prevent her from visiting Garsington during the weekend, but she is working extremely hard.
9	Is visited by Aldous Huxley.
12	Is visited by Fergusson with his drawings for 'Prelude'. Tells Brett her doctor will not allow her to go out. (This is Dr Ainger, a New Zealander.)
13	Gives all her news to JMM, including discussing her health, a process she repeats on 14 by which time Chaddie Beauchamp and their Aunt Belle have visited her. 'Miss Elizabeth Smith', a pastiche, is published in the *New Age*.
15	Another letter to JMM about their relationship, her health, her writing – and Dr Ainger.

Mid-month, tells VW how agonizingly her rheumatism is affecting her.

17	Informs JMM (and OM the following day) that her doctor has forbidden her to travel to Garsington for Christmas.
18	German planes again bomb London, something KM refers to in her correspondence.
20	By now JMM has briefly visited KM in London. They have agreed that she should go to the South of France.
21	Tells JMM that her pleurisy is exhausting her. She looks forward to living one day absolutely alone with him.

22	Informs Drey of the serious condition of her left lung: from now on she must be out of England every year between September and April otherwise she will become consumptive. Tells JMM she believes him to be a poet. She feels better but is quarrelling with LM.
23	In a letter concluded on 24 tells JMM she has learnt there is a spot on her right lung which makes her leaving England all the more imperative although the Hotel Beau Rivage, to which she asks him to write, must not be told of her condition. She wishes that they were married.
24	Feels better, she tells JMM, but her temper is bad now and she takes it out of LM. Asks when her passport will be ready. Thanks OM and her daughter Julian for their Christmas presents.
25	KM and JMM spend Christmas Day apart, she in her new flat, he at Garsington although he soon returns to London.
28	Asks OM if she can travel to Garsington on New Year's Day prior to leaving an England she now finds horrible. Everything has changed for her. Shops with JMM in London.

1918

EVENTS, THE ARTS, LITERATURE: U.S. President Wilson's 14-point peace plan (Jan.); U.K. vote is given to married women over 30 (Feb.); murder of the Tsar and his family (July); influenza pandemic reaches Britain (Sept.); armistice ends the Great War (Nov.); deaths of Debussy (March), Wilfred Owen (in action) (Nov.) and Apollinaire (Nov.); Willa Cather publishes *My Antonia*; Wyndham Lewis, *Tarr*; Strachey, *Eminent Victorians*; Rebecca West, *The Return of the Soldier*.

January

1 (Tues)	Travels with JMM to Garsington.
c.4	Returns to London, staying as a guest of Chaddie Beauchamp's at the Empress Club, Dover Street.
7	Sets out alone for Bandol as the Foreign Office has refused LM a travel permit.
8	Arrives from Southampton in Le Havre at 10 a.m., leaving for Paris late afternoon.

9	Arrives in Paris in the early hours, later describing her journey so far to JMM before boarding the train for Marseilles.
11	Describes to JMM her terrifying experiences at Marseilles station before her Bandol train left. At Bandol the Hotel Beau Rivage, in which she stayed in December 1915, has changed hands and no one remembers her.
12	Records in her notebook that she feels slightly better and should be able to write soon.
15	Describes her eventful journey to Bandol to Fergusson and, on 18, to AB and OM.
20	Assures AB of her happiness once she is married to JMM.
25	After reading his poem 'To my dear friends' tells JMM he will be the great poet of the age.
26	Makes it clear to JMM that she does not want LM with her.
27	Is dissatisfied with her current writing.
30	Admits her homesickness to JMM and is desperate to hear from him, particularly after the recent air raid on London. Begins (or 31) 'Je ne parle pas français'.

February

By now KM is receiving £208* p.a. (£4 a week) from HB.

3 (Sun)	Describes to JMM her 'two kick offs' to writing: one is real joy, a sense of being at peace and the other a 'cry against corruption' in its widest sense. Meanwhile she cannot forget the war which is poisoning everything.
4	Posts the first part of 'Je ne parle pas français' to JMM. Her night fears continue.
7	Finds Bandol very stimulating for her writing, she tells JMM.
8	JMM professes to be overwhelmed by the first part of 'Je ne parle pas français'.
9	Is delighted with JMM's reaction to the opening of her story but depressed by the politicians at Versailles.
10	Dreams a story, even including the title 'Sun and Moon', and immediately writes it down. Finishes 'Je ne parle pas français'. At the same time is horrified by the prospect of LM's arrival, wondering if JMM is ill and she is coming to tell her.

12	Uninvited LM arrives in Bandol, much to KM's fury. She is about to start work on 'Bliss'.
14	Believes LM is annoyed that her health is all right and not in the crisis which prompted her (LM's) journey. She also tells JMM she is now dissatisfied with her work prior to 'Je ne parle' and must 'reconstruct everything'.
19	First haemorrhage of the lungs: records in her notebook spitting blood every time she coughs. Fears she may have galloping consumption and be unable to finish her work, leaving only 'scraps'. At the same time makes light of her condition to JMM although admitting it will prolong her stay in Bandol.
20	Declares how much she wants to be with JMM in England seeing a 'good lung specialist', not with LM in Bandol and a 'very shady medicine man'.
22	Tells OM that the beautiful spring has made her feel the world's corruption all the more.
23	Pours scorn (in a letter to JMM) on Yeats and his attitude to Keats.
25	Admits to JMM her 'acute exasperation' and 'black rage' with LM.
27	Quoting Shakespeare's *A Winter's Tale*, makes clear to JMM her adoration of the English language.
28	Completes 'Bliss' and sends it to JMM.

March

1 (Fri)	Assures JMM that she is much, much better.
3	Notes to JMM that they are even using the same words in their appreciation of Wordsworth.
5	Tells JMM she feels 'steeped in Shakespeare'.
10	JMM writes KM a detailed criticism of 'Bliss' to which KM replies on 14.
13	Is open to JMM about her LM complex but admits on 16 that she wants her to travel back to England with her as she would be so helpful.
16	Begins to experience difficulties in obtaining permission to travel back to England.
18	JMM reports that 44 pages of 'Prelude' have now been printed.

18–19   In Marseilles, staying at the Hotel de Russie to see the British Consul, the police and Cooks about her return journey, gives JMM an account of these visits and her (optimistic) travel plans, before returning to Bandol.

21   Leaves for Marseilles. She feels ill and intimidated by the journey ahead. LM loses all her own luggage.

22   Arrives in Paris with LM to discover that the authorities will not allow her to travel on for a week or more. Finds a hotel next to the Sorbonne and informs JMM of their new address (Select Hotel, 1 Place de la Sorbonne).

23   Experiences at first hand the long-range shelling of Paris which begins today.

26   Tells JMM she is in Hell rather than Paris, with LM as a 'fiend-guardian' and, on 28, that she would not survive without the thought of him.

30   Graphically describes the German bombardment of Paris to JMM.

31 (Easter Day) With LM works in a canteen beneath the Gare du Nord to pass the time safely. But the experience exhausts her and she will not repeat it, even if LM will.

April

3 (Wed)   Receives permission to return to England but still has to await a boat. Meanwhile feels utterly helpless.

6   Tells JMM that there is a chance she will travel across on 10.

8   Puts on record for JMM the complete indifference of all the English officials whom she has met in Paris. She is moving to a hotel at Gare St Lazare as she dare not risk a last-minute dash across Paris with all the shelling and raids.

10   Leaves Paris.

11   Arrives in London and stays with JMM at 47 Redcliffe Road. Between now and mid-May they are visited by the Morrells. The visit is not a success.

17   Ainger confirms consumption but agrees that a sanatorium would be no good for KM who warns LM of the highly contagious nature of her disease on 18.

26   Records in her notebook that she would like to stay at Redcliffe Road until the end of the war.

May

3 (Fri)   As soon as the decree nisi becomes absolute marries JMM at Kensington Register Office, Marloes Road. Brett and Fergusson are the witnesses.

6   AB writes to Clara Palmer (an old family friend of the Beauchamps) telling her that KM has at long last learnt to love her parents and is writing sweet letters to them. If she has missed out in life, however, it is her own fault.

9   Lunches with the Woolfs. VW reports that she appears extremely ill. KM's unsigned review of *Paris Through an Attic* by A. Herbage Edwards appears in the *TLS*.

12   Praises to Brett VW's seriousness and honesty about writing.

14   Tells VW how much she likes her story 'The Mark on the Wall'.

16   JMM gives KM a two-volume edition of Dorothy Wordsworth's *Journal*.

17   Travels to the Headland Hotel, Looe, Cornwall, a booking which Drey has made for her, and is quickly praising the hotel and the kindness of the staff to JMM.

20   Reports to JMM that she is recovering from the pleurisy she had in London but admits to LM that her left lung is giving her terrible pain and she feels very ill although exquisitely looked after. JMM makes it clear she need not review books unless she wants to. Nevertheless he sends her a book which the *Times* sent him.

21   Tells JMM she is anxious to review books. The sea and coastline remind her of New Zealand.

23   Acutely accuses JMM of being happier and flourishing more when they are not together. They could carry on their correspondence and send each other work.

24   Describes to OM her first walk since arrival. She is by no means positive about everything she saw and loathes hotels. To JMM comments acidly on the vileness of people, including even children.

25   Makes it clear to JMM that she does not want a house in London. He sends her Dostoevsky's *Possessed* and a French book for review.

26   Criticizes Gissing's *Eve's Ransom* in a letter to JMM.

27	Reassures JMM, after his reaction to her letter of 23, that he means everything to her.
28	Tells JMM she believes the locals think that she and Drey are spies.
29	Suggests to VW that Cornwall is preferable to the South of France for artists. Informs JMM that the Woolfs dislike Fergusson's drawings for 'Prelude'. He is not to bother with 'Carnation' (a story she has just written and sent to him). Writes four prose poems 'To a Butterfly', 'Foils', 'Le Regard' and 'Paddlers'. Despite her telling JMM on 30 that she cannot write them as verse, 'The Butterfly' (sic) does exist as verse.
31	Suggests to LM that the three of them should after all have the 'Elephant' (their nickname for a house they have in mind in Hampstead) and try to live in harmony there.

May–June (whilst at Looe), writes a series of pieces which exist both as free verse and as prose: 'Strawberries and the Sailing Ship', 'Malade' (prose title: 'Pulmonary Tuberculosis'), 'Pic-Nic', 'Arrival' (prose title: 'Hotels') and 'Dame Seule'.

June

1 (Sat)	Believes the agents for the Hampstead property are putting pressure on JMM because they realize he is keen to acquire it, she tells him.
3	Suggests to JMM that, as she does not want to hurt Fergusson's feelings about his 'Prelude' designs, perhaps both kinds should be printed.
5	Trenchantly criticizes Hardy's *The Well Beloved* to JMM.
6	Tells VW that in her present circumstances she feels the writing business is wonderful. KM's unsigned review of René Benjamin's *Le Major Pipe et son père* appears in the *TLS*.
8	Vents her fury on LM for discussing her and her health behind her back, in particular with Mr Gwynne. (He is the foreman of the factory in which LM works. The outcome of the discussion has been the suggestion that she enter a sanatorium.) In contrast, her letter to JMM expresses her total love for him and ascribes her 'blackness' to her illness.

16	Tells LM that she is now suffering from extremely painful spinal rheumatism and feels cursed by her perpetual ill health. Describes to JMM the kindnesses of Mrs Honey (the old woman looking after KM at the Headland Hotel): she has reconciled her not only to England but to mankind too.
17	Drey begins to paint KM. (This is the portrait which is now in Te Papa, Wellington.)
20	Expresses her deep homesickness for New Zealand in her notebook.
21	Is joined by JMM at the Headland Hotel.
24	VW sets up the last words of 'Prelude'.
26	Tells LM that at the moment she is fond of her.
29	Returns with JMM to 47 Redcliffe Road, London.

July

4 (Thurs)	KM's unsigned review of Paul Margueritte's *Pour toi, patrie* appears in the *TLS*.
5	Addresses Chekhov directly in her notebook and, around this time, complains of the difficulty which she has in writing down the stories that are all ready in her head. Leonard Woolf prints off the last of 'Prelude', leaving only the title page and dedication still to be done.
10	The Woolfs glue, cover and send out the first copies of 'Prelude'.
11	'Prelude' is published (c.300 copies).
12	VW, despite some criticism of it, finds 'Prelude' to be a 'work of art'.
13	JMM is highly critical of Sassoon's *Counter-attack and Other Poems* in the *Nation*. This causes turmoil at Garsington.
15	Reveals to LM that the *English Review* is going to pay her £6 6s.* for 'Bliss'.
16	Tells OM that she longs for a body which is not her enemy trying to break her spirit.
22	The *Continental Times*, a German English-language newspaper, reprints 'A Pic-Nic' as 'An English Pic-Nic, A Study of the Middle Class Mind', using it as anti-British propaganda.

August

'Bliss' is published in the *English Review*.

1 (Thurs)	Admits to LM that her nature is affected by the constant pain she is in.
2	Rheumatism forces KM to cancel a visit to Asheham.
7	Reading 'Bliss' VW feels that KM has ruined her reputation.
8	Death of AB. Reacting to the news, which she hears on 10, KM describes her as 'the most exquisite, perfect little being – something between a star and a flower'.
14	In relation to AB's death, tells Brett that she admires 'courage', 'spirit', 'poise' (all inadequate words) more than anything.
15	Again pays tribute to AB in a letter to OM and, about the same time, in one to VW.
17	Thanks Chaddie Beauchamp for letting her see some of AB's letters.
19	Tells OM that she hopes the electrical treatment which she is just about to have for her rheumatism will renew her.
c.23	Goes to stay at her Aunt Belle's house, the Old Vicarage, Tadworth, Surrey, for a few days.
25	Complains to Brett about the constant pain she is in.
26	Moves with JMM to 2 Portland Villas, East Heath Road, Hampstead, a property which they are renting.

September

During the month renews her friendship with Koteliansky from whom she has been estranged. Probably this month, as her health continues to be extremely poor, first approaches, on the recommendation of Drey, **Dr Victor Sorapure**, a consultant at Hampstead General Hospital.

5 (Thurs)	Is continuing with the electrical treatment for her rheumatism.
7	'Carnation' appears in the *Nation*.
20?	Records that in her fits of temper she is extremely like DHL.

October

5 (Sat)	Informs Brett that she has seen a specialist who has confirmed that both her lungs are affected and she cannot

	recover in London. Meanwhile she has typed 30,000 words of her 50,000-word book. (This is *BOS*.)
8	Discussing the death of the critic, Robert Ross (on 5), reveals her own horror of death to OM.
14	KM's 30th birthday. Prompted by his cousin HB, Sydney Beauchamp, an eminent doctor, examines KM and says she has no chance unless she enters a sanatorium.
21	Records that she finds her surroundings delightfully remote and peaceful.
22	Suggests to OM that England ought to be closed during the winter months and speculates that DHL's problem may be his lack of a sense of humour.
27	Confined to her bed, finds her circumstances hellish, but in the same letter to Brett admits how much she has enjoyed DHL's company recently. He is his old self. (DHL stayed in Hampstead 7–22 October.)

November

4 (Mon)	Is now suffering from neuritis, but manages to be witty about it. Unable to write, has read Meredith's *The Egoist* and *Rhoda Fleming*, admiring the former, disparaging the latter. DHL has sent her his latest play. (This is *Touch and Go*, written in October.)
6	Is visited by VW who describes her appearance a few days later: she is feeble and creeps about the room. The long story she has written (presumably 'Je ne parle pas français') is full of hatred.
7	Tells VW that she (VW) clearly lives for writing and that makes her very important to her.
13	VW tells Vanessa Bell that she finds KM, whom she will visit today, 'very interesting' despite 'Bliss', someone who 'cares about writing…the rarest and most desirable of gifts'.
17	Writes to OM that, given world events, she is depressed about the state of the world and people's lack of heart. She has been translating Gorki's *Journal of the Revolution*.
28	VW pays KM another of her weekly visits.

December

1 (Sun)	Has tea with Gertler who finds her much better.
5	DHL sends KM a book by Jung and stresses his own belief in friendship.
9	VW visits KM again.
10	DHL writes another friendly letter to KM, repeating his November invitation that she visit him at Middleton-by-Wirksworth, Derbyshire.
17	Deplores the state of her health to Brett. She feels so cold.
25	Arranges an enjoyable 'old-fashioned' Christmas during which she and JMM give a party which includes Koteliansky, Gertler and the Campbells. KM's last Christmas in England.

1919

EVENTS, THE ARTS, LITERATURE: Founding of Fascist Party in Italy (March); massacre at Amritsar (April); Germans sign peace treaty at Versailles (June); death of Renoir (Dec.); first performances of Elgar's Cello Concerto and Holst's 'The Planets'; Sherwood Anderson publishes *Winesburg, Ohio*; Eliot, *Poems*; Ronald Firbank, *Valmouth*; Pound, *Quia Pauper Amavi*; Shaw, *Heartbreak House*; VW, *Night and Day*.

January

Early in the year, at a salary of £800* p.a., JMM is offered the editorship of the *Athenaeum* which he takes up in February, leaving his job as Chief Censor at the War Office and appointing Aldous Huxley and **J.W.N. Sullivan** as assistant editors. His editorial office is at 10 Adelphi Terrace, The Strand.

11 (Sat)	Sorapure initiates a course of treatment by injections which leave KM with a high temperature for 48 hours every time they are applied.

February

20 (Thurs)	Invites VW to tea on 24. (The latter has been unaware that KM's health has continued to decline and that this is the simple explanation for her silence since November.)

March

7 (Fri)   As JMM begins a short holiday at Garsington, Sorapure tells KM that her life is too sedentary.

15   MS of 'A Suburban Fairy Tale' (published in *SCOS*).

22   VW visits KM, later confiding in her diary that although KM is in the thick of a literary profession, with a pile of books to review, she is in no sense a literary drudge. Above all she cares about writing, albeit very differently from VW herself.

April

4 (Fri)   KM's reviews of novels begin to appear in the *Athenaeum* (JMM's first number), also the first of thirteen instalments appearing at intervals of her own and Koteliansky's translation of Chekhov's letters.

7   Mentions to Koteliansky that there appears to be a 'rumpus' between her and DHL and FL, but her garden is too small for such large, prancing animals.

c.10   The birth of kittens to her cat prompts her to admit to VW that she would like to give JMM a baby.

11   Reviews *Christopher and Columbus* by Elizabeth Beauchamp and *What Not* by Rose Macaulay in the *Athenaeum*.

16   KM and JMM have tea with VW who finds the former much easier to talk to. Heinemann have rejected *BOS*.

18   In the *Athenaeum* reviews *Old Junk* by H.M. Tomlinson who then writes her an appreciative letter of thanks. Her poem 'Fairy Tale' signed 'Elizabeth Stanley' (her paternal grandmother's name which she uses for all her *Athenaeum* poems) also appears in this issue.

21   KM and JMM are visited by the Woolfs. The four mingle with the crowds on Hampstead Heath (it is Easter Monday) but, VW records, KM looks gaunt and does not enjoy the experience.

25   KM's poems 'Covering Wings' and 'Firelight' appear in the *Athenaeum*.

May

2 (Fri)   KM's sketch 'Perambulations', which seems to relate to her difficulties in finding publishers for her work, appears in the *Athenaeum*.

9	Reviews (critically) Maugham's *The Moon and Sixpence* in the *Athenaeum*. With JMM has tea with VW in Hampstead.
c.12	Tells VW she finds Eliot's *Poems* (published on 12 by the Hogarth Press) 'unspeakably dreary' and 'The Love Song of J. Alfred Prufrock' in fact a short story.
19	Records that she lives to write and asks only for time to write her books. In the next days writes brief bulletins detailing her appalling health.
23	Reviews Cannan's *Pink Roses,* signed KM (sic), in the *Athenaeum* which also includes her poem 'Sorrowing Love'. (KM had briefly and anonymously noticed *Pink Roses* in the *Athenaeum* on 16.)
After 23	Laments in her notebook the lack of such qualities as warmth, eagerness and high-spiritedness in JMM which, however, make no difference to her love for him. Their lack, however, in his country makes all the difference to how she regards it. England means nothing to her.
c.27	Admits to VW she is no poet and mentions Chekhov's distinction between a writer putting the question (his true vocation) and attempting to solve it. (Chekhov's letter, in which he develops this point, will be published in the *Athenaeum* on 6.6.)
29	With JMM throws a party (which she will find very dull). Amongst those present are St John Hutchinson, Frank Swinnerton, Roger Fry, Edward Dent, Clive Bell and Russell.
30	Reviews Daisy Ashford's *The Young Visiters or Mr Salteena's Plan* in the *Athenaeum*.

June

Probably this month records her hurt about JMM's neglect of her and concludes that he should not have married.

4 (Wed)	Suggests to VW that there is a 'certain *silliness*' about Forster who has recently visited her.
6	Enthuses to Koteliansky about Chekhov's 'wonderful' letters, making the same point about one of them that she made to VW c.27 May.
7	Is visited by OM.
9	Is visited by Brett.
13	Reviews VW's 'Kew Gardens' under the title 'A Short Story' (unsigned) in the *Athenaeum*.

16	Is visited by Brett and Gertler.
19	Fry dines with KM and JMM.
20	Reviews May Sinclair's *Mary Olivier: A Life* in the *Athenaeum*.
21	Fully discusses her health with Sorapure.
24	Sends 'The Little Primitives' to the *Nation* which does not print it. (Under the title 'See-Saw' it will be published in *SCOS*.)
27	Praises Emily Brontë's poetry to OM, particularly the poem beginning 'I know not how it falls on me'. She was a poet without a mask, unlike contemporary poets.
30	Has tea with Strachey, reading him parts of a letter from VW describing Garsington.

July

1 (Tues)	Attacks the sneering gossip-mongers, in a letter to OM, who never create anything and are the enemies of true art.
4	KM's poem 'A Little Girl's Prayer' appears in the *Athenaeum*. Has tea with VW whose sympathies extend to JMM.
11	Is visited by VW who records on 12 how much she enjoyed the visit and is liking KM more and more.
13	Powerfully denounces, in a letter to OM, all the preparations for celebrating the Versailles Peace Treaty [to be held on 19] when so many young men, like LB, now lie dead.
23	Having recently had tea with KM, VW tells a correspondent that she (KM) is probably going to San Remo soon. She has written stories which the Woolfs are thinking of printing.

By late July KM feels very ill again, her spirits not helped by the inclement weather. All she can do is work.

August

Early this month, mentions to Koteliansky that she finds it strange that ultra-modernists like Eliot and Joyce write as they do post-Chekhov.

8 (Fri)	Reviews Conrad's *The Arrow of Gold* in the *Athenaeum* in which the tenth instalment of her and Koteliansky's translation of Chekhov's letters also appears.

13	Admits to OM that she has felt so ill recently that she has decided to enter a sanatorium from September to April. She is now experiencing terrible headaches.
15	Reviews Hugh Walpole's *Jeremy* in the *Athenaeum*.

Mid-month, tells Koteliansky that above all she wants to be alone and to work.

16	Meets HB for the first time since March 1912. However, he and JMM do not see eye to eye and he does not raise KM's annual allowance beyond the £300* which it becomes at some point in 1919.
17	After a talk with Sorapure, who tells her she would not be able to work in a sanatorium, gleefully accepts the alternative plan of wintering on the Italian Riviera.
21	Praises as 'immortal' Chekhov's 'The Steppe' in a letter to Koteliansky.
22	KM's poem 'Secret Flowers' appears in the *Athenaeum*.

September

9 (Tues)	Writes a farewell letter to JMM, in case she dies suddenly, with instructions about the disposal of her belongings including her MSS which 'I simply leave to you'. (This letter is deposited at the Bank of New Zealand, Queen Victoria Street, and JMM does not receive it until after KM's death.)
10	Farewell meeting with HB.
c.14	Accompanied by JMM and LM sets off for San Remo on the Italian Riviera initially staying at the Villa Flora.
c.27	Moves to Casetta Deerholm, Ospedaletti. After she and LM have settled in, JMM returns to London.

Autumn, 'The Pictures' is published in *Art and Letters*.

October

1 (Wed)	Describes her present surroundings to Koteliansky, confirms the arrival of material relating to Chekhov from him and says she will begin work on it at once.
3	Strachey writes to say how much he admires KM's weekly reviews in the *Athenaeum*.
7	Although plagued by insects, reports to JMM that she feels much better.

10	Reviews Swinnerton's *September* in the *Athenaeum*. Casetta Deerholm obtains running water.
11	Manages to walk to Ospedaletti.
14	KM's 31st birthday.
17	Reviews Compton Mackenzie's *Poor Relations* and Cannan's *Time and Eternity* in the *Athenaeum*.
18	Visits San Remo.
20	Agonizes to JMM about the world's corruption that she comes across when believing 'all is fair'.
24	Reviews F. Brett Young's *The Young Physician* in the *Athenaeum*.
26	Tells JMM that the insects are a pest, making work very difficult.
31	Reports to JMM that her cough is very troublesome and she feels lonely and depressed. KM and Koteliansky's translation of Chekhov's letters conclude in the *Athenaeum*.

November

3 (Mon)	Hears indirectly that HB hates this coast and would like to be back in England.
4	Speculates to JMM that her depression may partly be a symptom of tuberculosis. All she wants to do is work.
6	Tells JMM that this must be their last separation; she could not bear another.
7	Reviews *Richard Kurt* by Stephen Hudson [i.e. **Sydney Schiff**] in the *Athenaeum*.
8	Criticizes Shaw's plays and prose in a letter to JMM. He is a concierge in literature's house, not actually living there. In fact for her only Dostoevsky, Chekhov and Tolstoy live there. In another letter to JMM on 8 emotionally tries to dissuade him from his proposal to give up the *Athenaeum*, borrow from HB, travel to Ospedaletti and replace LM in caring for her.
9	Richard Murry completes setting 'Je ne parle pas français'.
10	Tells JMM that she dislikes VW's *Night and Day* which she is currently reviewing. It omits the war but that war, she feels passionately, changes everything and must be faced.
11	Likes her new doctor, Ansaldi, who says she could be cured in two years.

12	Entertains HB, who gives her much love and attention, his cousin Connie Beauchamp and her friend Jinnie Fullerton. The visit goes well but they do not like Ospedaletti and recommend Menton.
13	JMM tells KM that her novel-reviewing in the *Athenaeum* is very well regarded.
16	Suggests to JMM that the novels which he is asking her to review are inadequate: they do not take account of the war which has altered everything. There must be a new perspective.
20	Rants to JMM about the horror of living with LM. She cannot write a book with her around.
21	Reviews VW's *Night and Day* in the *Athenaeum*. JMM has praised the review as a masterpiece but VW herself thinks she is being spiteful.
22	HB, who has been ill since visiting KM, leaves Toulon for Naples.
c.25	Reads about the Italian poet Guido Gozzano who had consumption and moods of black depression. (He died in his early thirties.)
26	Receives a telegram from HB in Naples: he is finally leaving for New Zealand. Tells JMM that she does not want the Woolfs to have any of her new work.
28	Reviews Dostoevsky's *An Honest Thief and Other Stories*, translated by Constance Garnett, in the *Athenaeum*.
30	Enviously compares her own lot with that of VW calmly writing in her own home with her husband nearby.

December

1 (Mon)	In a fever and depressed, tells JMM that she now distrusts Ansaldi. Sorapure is the only doctor whom she trusts.
4	Sends JMM her poems 'Et Après', 'He wrote' and 'The New Husband'. The latter comments directly on their relationship and deeply upsets him. Tells JMM she is thinking of adopting a baby boy as she cannot bear being so alone: their dilemma is that JMM must remain in England to keep the *Athenaeum* going as they need the money.
5	Stresses to JMM the importance of speaking for one's generation rather than saying one is doing so – which is

enfeebling. JMM's review of *Georgian Poetry, 1918–1919* in the *Athenaeum* savagely attacks the anthology.

8   Is examined by Dr Foster who gives her a bulletin on the state of her health: she has had slight bronchial pneumonia. Her left lung is seriously diseased, her right at the moment quiescent. She must first recover from the pneumonia. JMM makes clear how devastated he is by her letter of 4 and stoutly defends his behaviour. (In turn this letter, which KM finds egoistical and misunderstanding, evokes a violent response from KM. She writes on the back of the envelope that it has killed something within her and she no longer fears death.)

9   Gives good reasons why JMM who is deeply upset by her recent letters and poems and therefore wants to visit her should not do so. (This is the theme of KM's next letters and telegrams.) JMM asks her to forget his horrible letter of 8. Koteliansky urges her to think positively about her health.

13   Thanks Koteliansky for his letter of 9. She hopes to recover but if she dies she may go to a consumptives' heaven in which case she will meet Chekhov.

15   Analyses her state of mind and her relationship with JMM in her notebook. Her obsession with death has gone as has her desire to live in England or even, particularly, with JMM. Calls herself 'a dead woman'. Honesty is to be prized above everything else.

16   JMM arrives at Casetta Deerholm.

26   Reviews Alexander Kuprin's *The Garnet Bracelet* in the *Athenaeum*.

1920

EVENTS, THE ARTS, LITERATURE: Widespread violence in Ireland throughout the year; League of Nations inaugurated (Jan.); Bolshevism finally triumphs in Russia's civil war (Nov.); Knut Hamsun is awarded the Nobel Prize for Literature (Dec.); death of Modigliani (Jan.); the anti-art movement Dada is active in Europe; Colette publishes *Chéri*; Eliot, *The Sacred Wood*; Scott Fitzgerald, *This Side of Paradise*; Sinclair Lewis, *Main Street*; Owen, *Poems* (posthumous); Wharton, *The Age of Innocence*.

January

JMM is awarded the Order of the British Empire for his M.I.7 work during the war.

2 (Fri)	JMM leaves Casetta Deerholm to return to England.
4	Admits in her notebook to feeling very depressed in her surroundings as soon as the weather is bad. All she can do is work. JMM is back in London.
5	Sends JMM a long Chekhov letter with instructions, if he does not use it, to have it typed and sent to Koteliansky for the book they are writing. Begins her story 'Late Spring' (published as 'This Flower' in *SCOS)* and works hard at Chekhov. HB, having arrived in New Zealand on 4, marries Bright. KM hears the news on 10.
8	Records in her journal a day spent in hell. She must escape.
9	KM's poem 'Old-Fashioned Widow's Song' appears in the *Athenaeum*. The doctor's opinion is that her lung has improved, but her heart has not. She must leave Ospedaletti.
10	Thinks out her story 'The Exile', the title of which quickly changes to 'The Man Without a Temperament'.
11	Records her anguish that she and JMM are no longer as they were. 'These are the worst days of my whole life.'
12	Sends JMM 'The Man Without a Temperament', written in less than two days.
13	Tells JMM that her feelings towards LM have undergone a complete transformation and she now feels something like love for her. LM has also played her part in frightening off some unwanted nocturnal visitors who kept ringing their bell.
16	Begins her story 'A Strange Mistake', subsequently entitled 'The Wrong House' and published, apparently incomplete, in *SCOS*.
20	For OM recapitulates her time at Ospedaletti, her isolation, her moods, her relations with JMM and LM.
21	Leaves Ospedaletti and makes the difficult cross-country journey with LM to France, staying initially at L'Hermitage, a private nursing home in Menton.
22	Gives JMM the doctors' optimistic prognosis about her.
23	KM's poem 'A Sunset' (later 'Sunset') appears in the *Athenaeum* as does 'Anton Tchehov: Biographical Note' which

	is unsigned and written with Koteliansky. (The second part of this appears in the *Athenaeum* on 6 February.) Her relations with Connie Beauchamp and Jinnie Fullerton who live nearby are already excellent and she will never cut herself off from life again.
26	Asks JMM to send her stories, most of which she names, to the publisher Grant Richards.
29	Receives an 'abominably selfish' letter from JMM written on 26. The *TLS* reviews both 'Prelude' and 'Je ne parle pas français' (the latter, although dated 1919, will not be officially published by the Heron Press at Portland Villas until 15 February. Reprinted, with the last two paragraphs omitted, 46 words, in *BOS*).
31	In response to JMM's question 'How's money', and very hurt by it, details her recent and current expenditure and says she expected him to help her without her having to ask.

February

1 (Sun)	JMM tells KM that he will proceed with Constable as the publisher of her new collection of stories unless she is committed to Grant Richards.
2	Stresses to JMM that she must see the proofs of 'The Man Without a Temperament' before it is printed. Everything must be correct, every word right.
4	Admits to JMM that something has gone dead in her. He never listens to her explanations. Forbids republication of *IGP* as it is juvenile and not good enough. JMM informs her that Constable will publish her new collection on a 15% royalty and an advance of £40 on delivery of the MS.
5	Reminds JMM that, as she does not go out or see anybody else to talk to, he is her all.
6	DHL writes a violently offensive letter to KM. (He has just fallen out with JMM over articles which he submitted to the *Athenaeum*.)
7	Gives JMM the gist of DHL's letter and tells him to be proud and stop defending him.
8	Tells JMM she cannot have 'The Woman at the Store' reprinted as part of her new collection.

9	JMM suggests that *IGP* is an excellent early work and KM should allow it to be republished.
10	Notes to JMM the near identity of response by her and JMM to recent letters from DHL to them.
12	Tells JMM that if *IGP* is re-issued she must write an introduction as she is not proud of it.
15	Moves to the Villa Flora, Menton, to live with Connie Beauchamp and Jinnie Fullerton.
22	Experiences an enjoyable afternoon visit to Monte Carlo which, however, she finds hellish.

March

2 (Tues)	Tells JMM that, although her lungs and heart are much better, she is still tormented by rheumatism.
4	Informs LM that she intends to be received into the Roman Catholic Church.
14	Attempts to make it clear to JMM that she longs to be home just with him – and that means Portland Villas, nowhere else.
c.18	Briefly summarizes the state of her health for Drey: part of her left lung has gone which puts extra strain on her heart.
c.23	Celebrates, in a letter to JMM, the purity of artists like Chekhov, remote from all the corruption.
24	Reports on her health to JMM, saying that because of it HB must guarantee her her £300 p.a. for life.
c.29	After describing childhood memories of a vegetable garden, affirms her love of such gardens to Richard Murry.
c.30	Suggests to JMM that the rocks and stones of the South of France remind her of New Zealand.

April

1 (Thurs)	Writes to Sydney Schiff, who lives nearby, saying she would like to meet him. He calls on her on 2.
2	'The Diary of Anton Tchehov', translated by KM and Koteliansky, appears in the *Athenaeum*, as does Sullivan's review of 'Je ne parle pas français' under the title 'The Story-Writing Genius'.
4	Now agrees with JMM about Catholics: their duty is to a deity whereas hers is to mankind.

6	Visits Nice. Refuses point blank to agree to any changes in the text of 'Je ne parle pas français' for the book publication of the story.
7	Lunches with Sydney and Violet Schiff. Is now prepared to leave the alterations wanted by Constable [represented by Michael Sadleir] to the text of 'Je ne parle...' to JMM. She needs the money and JMM makes clear to her that she will not receive it unless Constable is satisfied with the text.
14	Is visited by the Schiffs who delight her and are giving a luncheon party for her. By now KM realizes that Sydney Schiff wrote *Richard Kurt*.
15	Visits the Oceanographical Museum and Aquarium in Monaco which bowls her over. Envies JMM going to see *Cymbeline* at Stratford-upon-Avon as she adores Shakespeare's pastoral world.
16	Agrees with JMM that Hardy is much greater than Henry James.
18	Tells JMM that she has paid a deposit for a flat for when she is next in the area. (This is in the Villa Isola Bella.)
24	Asks JMM to invite Eliot to supper on 2 May.
25	Seriously suggests to JMM that they hold their own Shakespeare festival.
c.28	Leaves Menton for Paris and thence London, rejoining JMM at 2 Portland Villas.

Spring, 'The Man Without a Temperament' is published in *Art and Letters*.

May

1 (Sat)	Drafts some of her story 'Revelations' and by 2 has nearly finished it.
4	Suggests to the Schiffs that her passion for life must be directed into work.
12	Attends a performance by the Spanish singer Raquel Meller at the Hippodrome.
14	Eliot and his wife Vivien come to dine. KM takes a dislike to the latter whose behaviour she immediately describes to the Schiffs. Reviews *The Vanity Girl* by Mackenzie in the *Athenaeum*.

15	'A Tragic Comedienne', an anonymous review of VW's *Night and Day*, appears in the *Nation*. It has been attributed to KM but this cannot now be proved.
28	Is visited by VW who ends up enjoying the meeting. Responds in the *Athenaeum* to a letter criticizing her review of Mackenzie's *The Vanity Girl* on 14.

June

2 (Wed)	Lunches with VW. They discuss writing for two hours.
4	Reviews *Potterism* by Macaulay in the *Athenaeum*.
10	Invites Drey to tea on 15.
11	'Revelations' appears in the *Athenaeum*, KM's first story to appear there (reprinted in *BOS*). Reviews *Growth of the Soil* by Hamsun in the *Athenaeum*.
25	Reviews *The Mills of the Gods* by Robins in the *Athenaeum*. Highly critical of it, KM produces by implication a statement about her own kind of fiction.

July

1 (Thurs)	Attends the first *Athenaeum* literary lunch launched by JMM. (VW is not impressed by it.)
2	Enthusiastically reviews *The Rescue* by Conrad in the *Athenaeum* in which KM's leader on the arrival of Mary Pickford and Douglas Fairbanks in London also appears.
3	Eliot tells Pound that JMM is much more tricky to deal with when KM is around. He believes her to be dangerous.
9	'The Escape' appears in the *Athenaeum* (reprinted in *BOS*) in which KM's critical review of Jane Mander's *The Story of a New Zealand River* also appears.
16	Reviews *The Happy Foreigner* by Enid Bagnold in the *Athenaeum* in which an enthusiastic unsigned review of a production of Chekhov's *The Cherry Orchard* also appears. (This is probably by JMM although attributed by him to KM after her death.)
17	Takes Richard Murry to see the Russian Ballet at the Royal Opera, Covent Garden.
25	Regrets lending Sydney Schiff *IGP* as she thinks poorly of it.

August

6 (Fri)   'Bank Holiday', KM's last story to be written in England, appears in the *Athenaeum* (reprinted in *GPOS*) as does her review of a new edition of *Esther Waters* by George Moore.

7   Tells Violet Schiff that their plans to go and stay in a hotel near Eastbourne have fallen through.

9   Cryptically records in her notebook her fury at the relationship between JMM and Brett (which has been developing for some time). KM is in bed again, unable to walk. All she wants is time to write her stories.

12   Records in her notebook that JMM cannot bear her coughing. Goes on to be highly critical of Brett and her relationship with JMM.

13   Reviews 'The Story of the Siren' by Forster in the *Athenaeum*, disliking his unwillingness to commit himself.

c.15   Tells Violet Schiff that she would love to talk for hours about Tolstoy.

19   Records in her notebook that JMM has revealed that he had considered taking rooms with Brett at Thurlow Road (where she lives) for the winter. KM is staggered at his selfishness.

20   Writes an unsigned leader on *The Autobiography of Margot Asquith* in the *Athenaeum*.

23   Remarks to Chaddie Beauchamp that she will not be returning to London in 1921; currently the weather is wintry. VW travels to London for a farewell visit to KM. She (VW) feels empty not having her to talk to.

27   'The Wind Blows' (a revision of 'Autumns: II') appears in the *Athenaeum* (reprinted in *BOS*) as does an unsigned leader on literary critics.

29   Tells Brett that she craves work but regrets her health.

September

13 (Mon)   Arrives at Isola Bella, Menton, after a contretemps in Paris in which KM and LM managed to lose each other.

15   Complains to JMM of 'pains and fever and dysentery'.

16   Having received £40* from LM, asks JMM to give the money to Sobieniowski who is demanding it for the return of some letters of hers. KM wants JMM to arrange every-

thing with a solicitor and Sobieniowski and for that to conclude all communication with the latter.

17   Tells JMM that she has never been so thin. [In April 1918, after being subjected to the German bombardment of Paris for three weeks, KM weighed seven stone, six pounds.]

21   Remarks to Sydney Schiff that she regards JMM as 'THE English Critic'.

23   Instructs JMM to burn everything he receives from Sobieniowski.

25   Finds in *BOS* [soon to be published] the triviality which she hates, comparing it unfavourably with Chekhov; dismisses much contemporary fiction comparing it unfavourably with Tolstoy.

October

Probably writes 'The Singing Lesson' (published in *GPOS*) this month after 'The Young Girl'.

1 (Fri)   'Sun and Moon' appears in the *Athenaeum* (reprinted in *BOS*).

4   Mentions to JMM the biblical story of the withered fig tree, having once seen one when with LM. Feels that there is a story buried underneath that, if only it could be dug out.

10   Makes clear to JMM that she deeply resents the relationship which has developed between him and Brett.

11   Having completed 'The Young Girl', immediately sends it to JMM calling it 'one of my queer hallucinations'.

13   Finds the novelist Bennett vulgar.

14   KM's 32nd birthday – which, to her dismay, JMM forgets.

15   Reviews *Three Lives* by Stein in the *Athenaeum* in which KM's review of *The Captives* by Walpole also appears. She doubts that he is a creative artist. As a result of this review Walpole writes to KM on 23. This in turn prompts a long but sympathetic letter from her explaining herself more fully on 27.

16   Examined by Dr Bouchage who is confident about KM's health although his prognosis is hedged with provisos. He too is a consumptive.

18   Recognizes in her notebook that her chief fault is not writing things out, not confronting problems as soon as

they occur. Also remarks on her love of order, everything being 'ship-shape'. Tells JMM that as her boat 'enters the dark fearful gulf' 'the greatest failing' would be to fear.

21   Believes that Connie Beauchamp and Jinnie Fullerton, who frequently visit her, may be offended that she has not converted to Catholicism.

28   Tells JMM that her iodine injections are making her extremely tired.

29   'The Young Girl' appears in the *Athenaeum* (reprinted in *GPOS*) as does KM's review of *A Gift of the Dusk* by R.O. Prowse which moves and influences her and of which the central character is a consumptive.

31   Admits to JMM that she falsifies slightly in her writing.

November

3 (Wed)   Sends the MS of her story 'The Stranger' to JMM. Puzzles LM by telling her that after her (KM's) death she will prove there is no immortality by sending her 'a coffin worm in a matchbox'.

6   Gives JMM a bulletin on her health, concentrating on her appalling headaches.

12   Writes 'Miss Brill'.

13   By now Jinnie Fullerton has accepted KM's offer to rent Villa Isola Bella for a year from 1 May 1921.

14   Telegraphs JMM to destroy the 1913 photograph of her which she particularly detests. (It has survived.)

17   Writes a lonely letter to JMM feeling that, unlike him, she has little time left.

18   Sends 'Poison', which she has just written, to JMM, carefully explaining it to him in a letter on 23. (JMM decides not to publish it in the *Athenaeum*.) Asks if J.B. Pinker is the best literary agent for her.

26   'Miss Brill' appears in the *Athenaeum* (reprinted in *GPOS*).

27   Is working on 'The Daughters of the Late Colonel' which, as it is long, is particularly suitable, she tells JMM, for serial publication.

28   Is cruelly suffering from the cold.

December

The New Keepsake for the Year 1921, edited by X.M. Boulestin, reprints 'The Black Cap'.

1 (Wed)	Tells Sydney Schiff that she reviews only for the money and would much prefer to do her own work instead. Praises Chekhov to him as she does to JMM. She would give the whole of Maupassant for one short story by him.
2	*BOS* is published by Constable. It will be widely reviewed in the next weeks and months.
3	Reviews *Back to Life* by Sir Philip Gibbs and *The Valley of Indecision* by Christopher Stone in the *Athenaeum*. (These reviews are omitted from KM's posthumous *Novels and Novelists*, 1930, edited by JMM.)
4	Wells writes to JMM praising *BOS*, particularly 'Prelude'. They have brightened his day.
6	Completes 'The Lady's Maid' and sends it to JMM, violently objecting at the same time to the way in which Constable has advertised her book and the paragraph on the paper cover. Now bitterly regrets cutting words from the book. About this time makes a detailed attack on DHL's *The Lost Girl* (published on 25 November).
8	By now Dr Bouchage has made her realize that she cannot continue with her reviewing. Informs JMM.
c.9	Tells JMM that she never wants to return to England, preferring instead to wander in the sun with him for the next ten years.
10	Reviews *In Chancery* by Galsworthy and *The Age of Innocence* by Wharton in the *Athenaeum*, noting that from the former, which is a continuation of *The Forsyte Saga*, the irony so evident in *The Man of Property* is all but gone. These are KM's last reviews in the *Athenaeum*.
12	Telegraphs JMM telling him to stop sending her 'false depressing letters' – he has just written to KM about his close relationship with other women, particularly **Elizabeth Bibesco**. In a letter remarks that she is not affected by what happens in his personal life. Above all else she wants to write.
13	In a burst of writing completes 'The Daughters of the Late Colonel', dedicating it to Dr Sorapure.

15	Unhappy and depressed, is cheered up by reading Chekhov's 'The Duel'.
16	*BOS* is reviewed in the *TLS*.
c.18	JMM leaves for Menton, arriving c.20.
19	Indirectly records, in an entry entitled 'Suffering', the agony she has experienced about JMM and Bibesco. The two good men she has known are Chekhov (dead) and 'unheeding indifferent' Sorapure. VW congratulates KM on the success of *BOS*.
24	'The Lady's Maid' appears in the *Athenaeum* (reprinted in *GPOS*).
26	Promises Drey that her next book will be better than *BOS* which she is sending her.
27	Replying to VW's letter of 19, says she would love to talk to her about writing, the only woman who can fulfil that role. In her notebook records that JMM is essential to her, for all his difference. They are two sides of a medal.
29	Sylvia Lynd reviews *BOS* positively in the *Daily News*.

1921

EVENTS, THE ARTS, LITERATURE: Germany reluctantly agrees to the level of war reparations (May); Irish Free State is formed (Dec.); Anatole France wins Nobel Prize for Literature (Dec.); death of Saint-Saëns (Dec.); De la Mare publishes *Memoirs of a Midget*; Aldous Huxley, *Crome Yellow*; DHL, *Sea and Sardinia*; Shaw, *Back to Methuselah*; Strachey, *Queen Victoria*.

January

'The Stranger' appears in the *London Mercury* which also carries a review of *BOS*.

7 (Fri)	JMM's review of *The Schoolmistress and Other Stories* by Chekhov, translated by Constance Garnett, appears in the *Athenaeum*. It may contain a contribution by KM.
11	JMM leaves for a short visit to England.
15	Desmond MacCarthy, reviewing *BOS* in the *New Statesman*, notes that the author's master is Chekhov.
17	Reveals to Richard Murry the extreme care she took in writing (for example) 'Miss Brill': the length of every sentence and the sound of every sentence had to be

absolutely right. Finally she read the whole story aloud a number of times until the expression of Miss Brill fitted her exactly. Her aim is that every word is in its place and no word can be omitted.

19	JMM arrives back at Villa Isola Bella.
21	De la Mare favourably reviews *BOS* in the *Athenaeum*.
23	J.C. Squire admiringly reviews *BOS* in the *Observer* giving KM advice for which she is grateful.

February

2 (Wed)	Tells OM that she has turned against the Riviera and the French. As for England, she never wants to see it again.
3	JMM leaves for England to wind up his business in London.
7	Tells Sadleir that she will give him first refusal of her new book which will comprise long short stories. She will never write a novel. She is poorly.
9	In a letter which KM has been meaning to write for some months profusely thanks Orage for all that he has taught her. (This letter eventually leads to their friendship being renewed.) Tells Waterlow that she and England 'simply don't get on'.
11	JMM's final number as the editor of the *Athenaeum* (on 19 it becomes the *Nation & The Athenaeum*). He hosts a farewell dinner which VW attends.
12	DHL, in a letter to Mary Cannan, asks her to spit on KM for him. She is a liar and she and JMM vermin.
13	VW sends a chatty letter to KM about contemporary writers but, it appears, does not receive a reply.
c.20	The American edition of *BOS* is published by Knopf. About this time JMM returns to Villa Isola Bella.
26	'Life of Ma Parker' appears in the *Nation & the Athenaeum* (reprinted in *GPOS*).

March

During this month, keeps some accounts of her expenditure.

Early this month, LM returns to England to arrange the removal from Portland Villas.

2 (Wed)	DHL, in a letter to Koteliansky, is abusive about KM and JMM.

11	Has a gland in her neck punctured and pus removed at the clinic of a Menton surgeon, Georges Leblanc. The operation will have to be repeated a few times.
13	Tells LM that she is staggered by JMM's meanness in not paying for her journey to and from Leblanc's surgery in Menton. What disturbs her especially is his lack of sensitivity.
14	Forecasts to LM that one day JMM will marry Brett because she gives him exactly what he needs from a wife: 'flattery, reverence, adoration'. Informs OM that she has been in bed for six weeks owing to her heart and lungs.
18	Bouchage again taps KM's neck. She thinks that he is becoming tired of her and, anyway, says she cannot stay in Menton beyond May. She is thinking of Switzerland and asks LM's help to travel there. She cannot rely on JMM.
20	Discusses JMM in a letter to LM: he will never finish with his affairs [i.e. with Brett and Bibesco]. She longs to be alone, free of him. Meanwhile her health is far worse than when she left England. Bouchage has failed her and she is now setting her sights on Switzerland and a course of treatment offered by a Dr Spahlinger.
24	Instructs Bibesco to stop writing love letters to JMM whilst she (KM) is living with him.

Late this month, makes clear to Waterlow her admiration of Eliot's *Prufrock*. She feels that is what she wants modern poetry to be.

April

Early this month, asks LM to regard her from now on not as a friend who needs looking after, but simply as a friend.

Mid-month, LM returns to Menton.

20 (Wed)	Tells Brett that she is now spitting blood. It is very cold and the house seems in chaos. She is pinning all her hopes on Switzerland.
23	'The Singing Lesson' appears in the *Sphere* (reprinted in *GPOS*).

End of the month, Dr Bouchage writes a lengthy medical report on KM.

May

'The Daughters of the Late Colonel' appears in the *London Mercury*. During this month, writes a long account for Sorapure about what it means to be tubercular.

4 (Wed)	Leaves Menton to travel with LM to Montreux, Switzerland. Meanwhile JMM goes to England to deliver some lectures on style at the University of Oxford.
7	From her hotel (Beau Site, Clarens-Montreux) describes for JMM her journey and the hotel.
11	Conrad Aiken reviews *BOS* in the *Freeman*: generally he is full of praise, but has some reservations.
14	Travels, on the spur of the moment, to Château Bellevue, Sierre, to consult a Dr Stephani, returning in the evening. He will not say that she will be cured, only that she still has a chance.
16	Feels certain that HB has cut her £300 p.a. allowance so sends his letter to JMM for him to open and tell her. (KM is wrong: her allowance remains.)
c.22	Tells OM that she has just paid Bouchage 2,000 francs* for his services and she is far worse than she was at Christmas. Her current literary passion is for Chaucer.
23	Defines her view of love for JMM: 'It is drawing out all that is finest and noblest in the soul of the other' and, on 24, reaffirms her absolute love for him.
26	Suggests to **Marie Belloc-Lowndes** that she cannot afford to die with so little written. Despite everything, she longs to praise life. 'I long, above everything, to write about *family love*...'. (See 'Who's Who... Belloc-Lowndes'.)

End of this month (or early June), moves to Pension du Lac, Sierre.

June

4 (Sat)	Admits to Brett that she is working against time.
9	JMM returns from London and joins KM at the Hotel Château Belle Vue, Sierre, to which she has just moved.
20	Remarks to Richard Murry that receiving daily nourishment from the likes of Chaucer, Shakespeare, Marlowe and Tolstoy is much better for her writing than reading lesser writers.

23	Following **William Gerhardie's** enthusiastic letter to her about 'The Daughters of the Late Colonel', thanks him and discusses the story.
c.24	Moves with JMM to the Palace Hotel, Montana.
25	Following JMM's visit to her, Elizabeth Beauchamp visits KM at Montana a few hours later.

Late this month (or early July), moves with JMM to Chalet des Sapins, Montana-sur-Sierre, which they rent. Elizabeth Beauchamp lives close by, at the Chalet Soleil, Randogne-sur-Sierre.

July

During the next four months writes several stories including, this month, 'Mr and Mrs Dove' (published in *GPOS*). Also begins stories which are never completed such as 'Susannah', and, this month, 'Such a Sweet Old Lady'. These unfinished stories will be published posthumously in *The Doves' Nest and Other Stories (DNOS)*, 1923.

22 (Fri)	Finishes 'An Ideal Family' (published in *GPOS*).
23	Records her dissatisfaction with 'An Ideal Family'. Wants to tackle 'a long story: "At the Bay", *with more difficult relationships'*.
24	Dismisses *Women in Love* (which has just been published in England), including her own depiction as 'Gudrun', in a letter to OM.
25	Writes 'Her First Ball' (published in *GPOS*). In a letter to Brett reiterates her hatred of England. She will never live there again.

August

4 (Thurs)	Is busy writing 'At the Bay'.
6	'Sixpence' appears in the *Sphere* (reprinted in *SCOS*).
11	Completes 'Marriage à la Mode' but records in her journal that she does not know how to write her next story ['The Voyage'] and is not helped by feeling so cold. LM leaves for London.
13	'Mr and Mrs Dove' appears in the *Sphere* (reprinted, slightly revised, in *GPOS*). JMM's review of *Women in Love*, which appears in the *Nation & the Athenaeum* under the title of 'The Nostalgia of Mr D.H. Lawrence' may have been written wholly or in part by KM.

14	Begins, and probably completes, 'The Voyage' (published in *GPOS*).
16	Asks J.B. Pinker, the literary agent, to act on her behalf.
20	Writes to LM that, since her departure, she has been ill with acute enteritis. 'An Ideal Family' appears in the *Sphere* (reprinted in *GPOS)*.
21	Admits to Chaddie and Jeanne Beauchamp that she cannot manage without LM.
23	Is working on 'A Married Man's Story' (published, unfinished, in *DNOS*).
26	Thanks Pinker for agreeing to be her literary agent.
27	Elizabeth Beauchamp visits but KM is too ill to see her.
29	In a wide-ranging letter to Brett mentions her health, the countryside which she is now living in, why she hates England, DHL's passion (which makes him a real writer, although KM is still critical of him), religion and contemporary love, and her own current writing.

September

Early in the month, in discussing her current writing, reveals to Pinker that she longs to write a novel. Remarks to Lynd that she has just completed six stories and is in the middle of a seventh. (This is 'At the Bay'.)

5 (Mon)	Tells Richard Murry that, with money made from her writing, she would like to build a small house near where they are living.
7	Proposes to LM, who has just returned from London, that she (LM) becomes her aide and companion, being paid £10*-£12* per month.
11	After hours of writing, completes 'At the Bay'.
12	Tells Brett that she has finished her book which will be called *At the Bay*. She has put all her effort into the title story which is a continuation of 'Prelude'. Meanwhile she is greatly enjoying the Cézanne book which Brett has lent her. Despite her lack of education in painting he seems to her to be the real thing.
14	Sends *At the Bay and Other Stories* to Pinker.
16	Drafts part of 'Second Violin' (published, unfinished, in *DNOS*).

24	Tells Sadleir, representing Constable, that she would like the firm to publish her new book. Remarks to Lynd that she dislikes VW's *Monday or Tuesday* stories as they are 'detached from life'.
29	Informs Pinker that she is accepting Constable's offer for her new book as long as he is satisfied with it.

October

1 (Sat)	In connection with her cousin Elizabeth Beauchamp, mentions to Brett how she delights in people's appearance. KM also finds her cousin's new novel *Vera* 'amazingly good'.
3	Returns to Pinker the signed agreement with Constable for the publication of her new book.
10	Informs both Pinker and Sadleir that she wants to add one story, 'The Garden Party', which she is just finishing, to her collection and call her new book by that title as it is more solid than the vague *At the Bay*.
14	KM's 33rd birthday. Thanks Jeanne for her birthday present, telling her she takes the greatest delight in reminiscing. Finishes 'The Garden Party' which JMM types in the next few days. Her notebook reveals about this time her own self-criticism: 'At the Bay' is not what it might have been; nor is 'The Garden Party' good enough.
18	Asks Koteliansky to tell her more about the Russian doctor whom he has mentioned to her. (This is Ivan Manoukhin who has a revolutionary way of treating tubercular patients.)
21	Responds positively to Gerhardie's request that she read his novel. (This is the so-far-unpublished *Futility*.) The only problem is that she lives so far away.
24	Thanks Aiken for his review of *BOS*, particularly for his comments on those stories in which she has failed. Remarks to Violet Schiff that she lives in the past and discusses some contemporary writing. Begins to draft 'The Doll's House'.
27	Lists stories for her next book [i.e. after *GPOS*], some of which KM works on about this time. They include 'Six Years After', 'Honesty', 'A Weak Heart' and 'Widowed', all of which are published, unfinished, in *DNOS*, the penultimate as 'Weak Heart'.

30   Completes 'The Doll's House' (published, revised, in *DNOS*).

November

Early in the month, begins to draft 'Six Years After'.

1 (Tues)   Writes to HB. KM's tone is fearful and apologetic; she says that she has been tortured by the thought that he grudges her the allowance of £300* p.a.

2   Sends Pinker 'The Doll's House'.

5   Reviews *To Let* by Galsworthy, a continuation of *The Forsyte Saga*, in the *Daily News*.

11   Emphasizes to Brett the immense effort she put into 'The Daughters of the Late Colonel'. It has been misunderstood, however; even Hardy wanted more about the sisters.

12   Sends Gerhardie a detailed critique of *Futility* as a result of which he overhauls the novel.

13   Urges herself to write, not to procrastinate, so that she fulfils her deepest wish to be a writer with an achieved body of work.

21   Begins to write 'The Weak Heart' (sic). Suggests to Gerhardie that Cobden-Sanderson might publish *Futility* and offers assistance in securing this. [He does publish the novel, in 1922.] She is not a highbrow and likes unfashionable things, examples of which she proceeds to give.

26   Begins a draft of 'Daphne' (published, unfinished, in *DNOS*).

28   'Her First Ball' appears in the *Sphere* (reprinted in *GPOS*).

29   Again asks Koteliansky for information about Manoukhin's treatment. Asks Sadleir to drop 'Sixpence' from *GPOS* and dispose of it, as she now regards it as sentimental. (It does not appear in *GPOS* but is included in *SCOS*.)

December

2 (Fri)   *Note-book of Anton Chekhov* translated by S.S. Koteliansky and Leonard Woolf is published by B.W. Huebsch of New York. (This is a revision of the translation which appeared in the *Athenaeum* on 2 April 1920, but no acknowledgement of KM's help is made.)

3	Tells Sydney Schiff that she has begun some novel reviewing again [in the *Daily News*] but the rubbish that she is sent dispirits her. Is also highly critical of the DHL of *Sea and Sardinia*, George Santayana, Anatole France and Pound. She intends to leave Switzerland: she cannot bear the Swiss peasantry.
4	Writes to Manoukhin in French asking him if he will accept her as his patient. Reveals to Koteliansky that she has not walked properly for over a year.
5	In a letter to Brett recalls seeing some Van Gogh paintings at an exhibition ten years ago which taught her something about writing: 'a kind of freedom – or rather, a shaking free.'
9	Referring to her long letter of 3, Sydney Schiff tells Vivien Eliot that he finds KM's personality fascinating.
c.15	Tells Elizabeth Beauchamp that all that is keeping her and JMM from despair, given the cold and lack of interesting letters, is the brilliance of Jane Austen.
19	Tells Brett about the problems which she is having in contacting Manoukhin – LM failed by telephone on 18. She must have a miracle, however, to give her hope.
c.20	Suggests to OM that Proust, whom they have been reading this autumn, 'is by far the most interesting living writer'.
23	Hears from Manoukhin and immediately tells Koteliansky that she will travel to Paris as soon as she is well enough.
24	'The Voyage' appears in the *Sphere* (reprinted in *GPOS*).
25	Reveals to Schiff her plans to see Manoukhin in Paris as soon as she can and then return there in May for a full course of treatment. She hopes for a complete cure. KM has re-read Joyce's *A Portrait of the Artist as a Young Man* and finds it very good. She and JMM will buy *Ulysses* as she now feels Joyce is immensely important and representative of the new novel, however off-putting some of his words and expressions.
26	Thanks Drey for the coat which she has sent her. Tells Brett that she will have to work hard to make the money for all the costs involved in receiving the Manoukhin treatment.
31	'Marriage à la Mode' appears in the *Sphere* (reprinted in *GPOS*). Returns to the subject of Joyce in a letter to

Sydney Schiff, qualifying her remarks of 25. She now understands the importance DHL attaches to friendship; the problem is one's pride.

1922

EVENTS, THE ARTS, LITERATURE: Disturbances (which lead to civil war) break out in Ireland (March); Mussolini becomes dictator of Italy (Oct.); the tomb of Tutankhamun is discovered (Nov.); Niels Bohr wins the Nobel Prize for Physics for his work on the structure of the atom (Dec.); death of Proust (Nov.); Eliot publishes *The Waste Land*; Hardy, *Late Lyrics and Earlier*; Joyce, *Ulysses*; DHL, *Aaron's Rod* and *England, my England*; Edith Sitwell, *Façade* (performed in public with music by William Walton in 1923); VW, *Jacob's Room*.

January
'At the Bay' appears in the *London Mercury* (reprinted, revised, in *GPOS*).

1 (Sun)	Begins 'The Doves' Nest' (published, unfinished, in *DNOS*).
4	Asks Brett if she minds shopping for her. Reads much of *Cosmic Anatomy* (by Dr Lewis Wallace) and finds it mind-enlargening.
7	HB receives KM's letter of 1 November 1921, writing across the top of it on 9 that he has never begrudged his children any of the allowances which he has paid them, regarding helping them, on the contrary, as a pleasure and a privilege.
11	Hears that the *Dial* has accepted 'The Doll's House'. Writes 'A Cup of Tea' in four to five hours (published in *DNOS*). After a visit from Elizabeth Beauchamp, whose appearance she ridicules, feels a falsity in their relationship.
12	Records in her notebook her desire to adopt a Russian baby and call him Anton.
15	Receives a letter from Elizabeth Beauchamp which makes her ashamed of her negative thoughts and comments of 11.
17	Confides to her notebook that writing a story is like a race 'to get in as much as one can before it *disappears*'.

21   Speculates over the whereabouts of a photograph of her grandmother as a young woman with her husband. KM would love to write lengthily about her. (The photograph has survived.)

24   Once she starts it, writes 'Taking the Veil' in about three hours (published in *DNOS*).

26   Records that she feels remote from Vera and Jeanne Beauchamp and would not mind if she never saw the former again. Hates her 'assumed cheerfulness'.

27   Is visited by Elizabeth Beauchamp. Suffers pain the whole day.

29   Tidies her papers and is pleased to destroy much: 'Whenever I prepare for a journey I prepare as though for Death. Should I never return all is in order.'

30   Is informed by Pinker that the *Westminster* has accepted 'The Garden Party'. Leaves Sierre with LM for Paris.

31   Arrives in Paris and takes a suite of rooms with LM at the Victoria Palace Hotel, 6 Rue Blaise Desgoffe. In the afternoon visits Manoukhin's clinic. He examines her and recommends that she start his treatment (which involves irradiating her spleen with X-rays) immediately. In a letter to JMM, completed early the following day, discusses the pros and cons of this and the implications for both of them. (The cost is 4,500 francs* for the first 15 sessions.)

February

1 (Wed)   Sees Manoukhin again, this time, as she has requested, with his French partner Dr Donat. They both describe the treatment and assure KM of its success and lack of risk. Privately believes that Manoukhin is both a good man and an 'unscrupulous impostor'.

2   JMM urges KM to start the treatment at once. Tells her Cassells have bought 'A Cup of Tea' for £10 10s.

3   Informs Manoukhin by telephone of her decision to start the treatment at once, then visits the clinic where Manoukhin assures her that she is absolutely curable.

4   'The Garden-Party' (sic) begins to be serialized in the *Saturday Westminster Gazette* (reprinted, revised, in *GPOS*). 'The Doll's House' is published in the *Nation & the Athenaeum* (reprinted in *DNOS*).

6	Mentions in her notebook Brett's beautiful letter which she has just received; JMM's apparent lack of concern about her now that he is by himself again and her belief that ultimately she must be cured mentally as well as physically.
7	Tells JMM that she has finished with cities for good, remarking to Elizabeth Beauchamp on 8 that what she objects to about Paris is the people.
8	Makes clear to JMM the deep offence she has taken to his letter of 5 in which he puts his work before her health. So she does not want him to join her. JMM writes to say that he is coming to Paris. Hears that the *Sketch* has accepted 'Taking the Veil'. Remarks to Gerhardie, from whom she has just heard, that, of her stories, the only ones that satisfy her to some extent are 'The Daughters of the Late Colonel' and parts of 'Je ne parle pas français'.
11	Is joined by JMM in Paris. The *Saturday Westminster Gazette* continues its serialization of 'The Garden Party'.
13	Feels extremely ill, in great pain and unable to do anything except lie down. Also feels without hope.
18	The *Weekly Westminster Gazette* concludes the serialization of 'The Garden Party'.
20	Completes 'The Fly', wholly written this month.
21	Describes to Elizabeth Beauchamp a woman in a room opposite who 'has a wicker cage full of canaries'. KM would like to offer her (Elizabeth) a good story one day.
22	'Taking the Veil' appears in the *Sketch* (reprinted in *DNOS*).
23	*GPOS* is published by Constable.
26	Gives this date to a draft of the fragmentary story 'The New Baby'.

March

During this month, tells Pinker that she is planning a series of linked stories which will form the third part of a narrative beginning with 'Prelude' and continued with 'At the Bay'. (KM does not realize until near the end of this month that J.B. Pinker died in February. On 29 she begins corresponding with Eric Pinker who has taken over his father's literary agency in Europe.)

2 (Thurs)   Deplores the Paris weather in a letter to Gerhardie thanking him for the letters to which she has been too ill to reply. She is ashamed of being ill.

3   Describes her and JMM's living and working conditions to Richard Murry and, in a later letter to him, reveals that only now does she understand what she wants to do in her work. She is satisfied with very little so far except 'The Daughters of the Late Colonel'.

6   Thanks Elizabeth Beauchamp for her generous letter about *GPOS* but hopes to make her next book better.

7   Tells LM that she has been planning a visit to New Zealand with JMM but knows it will remain a dream. Clement Shorter, of the *Sphere*, wants more stories from her.

9   Enthuses to Brett about the artistic nature of the French and attacks Bolshevism. She is revolted whenever she sees a picture of Lenin.

13   Reveals to Gerhardie that she felt possessed by the events which she was describing as she wrote 'The Voyage'.

18   Tells HB that she regards him as the soul of generosity and that she thanks God she was born in New Zealand. The *Nation & the Athenaeum* publishes 'The Fly' (reprinted in *DNOS*).

20   Reveals to Vera Beauchamp that, should her present course of treatment be unsuccessful, she is prepared to try a psychotherapeutic cure. VW tells a correspondent that she does not intend to read *GPOS*, describes her dislike of *BOS* and is admittedly malicious about JMM.

22   Briefly recapitulates for Sarah Gertrude Millin her life since 1903. Only in the last few years have her thoughts constantly returned to New Zealand and her early life there, which is what she really wants to write about, drawing 'upon one's real *familiar* life…Our secret life…'

24   Remarks to Elizabeth Beauchamp she has not been out of the hotel since her arrival except to go to the clinic and back. Now it is snowing. Refers to the savage review *GPOS* received in *Time and Tide* (on 3).

29   With JMM meets Joyce, having struggled through *Ulysses* which JMM will review in the *Nation & the Athenaeum* on 22 April. (The Schiffs organized the meeting and later Violet remarked that Joyce thought KM seemed to under-

stand the book better than JMM, although she herself later told Violet that she felt out of her depth discussing it.) Recommends to Richard Murry Goethe's *Conversations with Eckermann* as a book which becomes part of one's life.

30   Admits to Brett that she is not the slightest bit better.

April

4 (Tues)   Tells Brett that she admires Wyndham Lewis's art but he is lacking a real centre which KM explains as the working of the mind and soul together.

29   'Honeymoon' appears in the *Nation & the Athenaeum* (reprinted in *DNOS*).

May

'A Cup of Tea' appears in the *Story-Teller* (reprinted in *DNOS*).

1 (Mon)   Remarks to Brett that she appreciates the complexity of *Ulysses* whose Bloom and Marion Bloom are superb creations.

3   Readies herself to begin writing for Shorter's *Sphere*, 12 'spasms' of 2,000 words each.

10   With the weather much improved, spends an enjoyable day with the Schiffs in the Bois de Boulogne.

11   Tells LM that the Manoukhin treatment appears to be completely successful. Asks her to go down to the Hotel d'Angleterre, Randogne, to take rooms for her and JMM for the early summer. This LM does, calling in briefly to see KM in Paris on her way back to England.

26   First American edition of *GPOS*.

Late this month, meets Ivan Bunin who knew Chekhov but is disappointingly unwilling to discuss him with KM.

June

Gerhardie sends a copy of *Futility* to KM who urges him to continue writing in the same way. HB arrives in London and stays until September.

4 (Sun)   With JMM leaves Paris for Hotel d'Angleterre, Randogne. As KM describes to both LM and Brett on 5, everything goes wrong from the very beginning of the journey to the very end. She soon succumbs to pleurisy and a bad cold.

5	Suggests to Elizabeth Beauchamp that JMM needs a different kind of wife.
7	Desperately tired and virtually as ill as ever, asks LM to return to her as a companion secretary but in such a way that the initiative seems to come from her (LM). She says that JMM is completely uncomprehending. LM immediately responds.
13	Is visited by Elizabeth Beauchamp.
14	Asks LM to come as soon as she reasonably can and to believe in her love and her need for her as her wife. Tells Gerhardie that she hated writing 'The Fly' (which he disliked) but is enjoying writing 'The Doves' Nest' which makes her lead a double life: at the same time her own in her present circumstances but also that of her character, Milly.
24	Suggests to the young writer Arnold Gibbons that in his stories the influence of Chekhov is obstructing his own expression.
26	Envies HB his voyage on such a huge ship as the *Aquitania* and reminiscences about their voyage on the *Niwaru*.
29	Has a long talk with Elizabeth Beauchamp who has called to say goodbye. KM now travels with LM down to Sierre, staying at the Hotel Château Belle Vue again, leaving JMM at the Hotel d'Angleterre, Randogne.

July

During this month, writes the poem 'The Wounded Bird'.

5 (Wed)	Tells JM that the actual experiences of Brett [who is staying with KM in Sierre and whose visit she has eagerly anticipated] is extremely chastening.
7	Writes her last completed story, 'The Canary' (published in *DNOS*), as a present for Brett.
9	Mentions to HB that, whilst writing about a canary, she almost felt that she was living in a cage herself.
10	Discusses Chekhov with Gerhardie: he did *not* require medical training to write 'The Party'; he was obsessed with time, with wanting to live but at the same time to write.
13	Suggests to Gibbons that he has not yet made the influence of Chekhov his own in his stories.

| 17 | Tells Koteliansky that in contemporary writing she finds very little to help her in her own search for style. |

August

7 (Mon)	Writes an informal testament in a farewell letter to JMM asking him to 'Have a clean sweep…and leave all fair'.
9	Mentions Gerhardie to Violet Schiff and her liking for DHL's latest novel, *Aaron's Rod*. Her future plans are very vague.
10	Tells HB that she is so worried about her heart that she must see Sorapure as soon as possible.
12	JMM's review of DHL's *Aaron's Rod* and Gerhardie's *Futility* appears in the *Nation & the Athenaeum* under the title 'Two Remarkable Novels'. KM may have had some input as she wrote to JMM earlier this month suggesting she tone down his effusiveness a little.
14	Makes her formal will leaving specific possessions to friends and relations and instructing JMM to 'publish as little as possible and to tear up and burn as much as possible. He will understand that I wish to leave as few traces of my camping ground as possible.'
15 (or 16)	Leaves Sierre with JMM and LM, arriving in London on 17 and staying at Brett's house, 6 Pond Street, Hampstead. (JMM is next door.)
18	Consults Sorapure and immediately reports on this visit to HB.
21	Lunches with HB, Chaddie and Jeanne Beauchamp.
26	Tells Gerhardie that she is pleased to be back in London but dislikes the solemnity of the intelligentsia.
30	Lunches with Orage at Pond Street, describing her dissatisfaction with the life she has so far led in which, however, she has seen gleams of other possibilities.

September

Meets Koteliansky on a number of occasions. The two have been working since August on the translation of Maxim Gorki's *Reminiscences of Leonid Andreyev* (published 1928, New York; first English edition 1931). Continues radiation treatment with a London radiologist, Dr Webster, until the end of the month.

1 (Fri)	Spends the weekend with JMM at Vivian Locke-Ellis's house, Selsfield, Sussex. JMM stays on, visiting KM at weekends.
4	Tea with HB, the first of several social occasions with him during the month.
5	Meets Orage again (and also on 10). They discuss the occult theories of **P.D. Ouspensky** and **George Gurdjieff** as both are coming to believe that the healing of the body depends on spiritual health.
8	Lunches with Edward Garnett.
14	Attends a lecture given by Ouspensky at 28 Warwick Gardens.
15	Sees Sorapure.
17	Lunches with the Schiffs and Wyndham Lewis but the occasion is spoilt by the latter's offensiveness about Gurdjieff.
20	Receives a postcard sent by DHL on 15 August from Wellington containing the single word 'Ricordi' (=memories).
21	Has tea with Chaddie Beauchamp, and again on 24.
27	Writes to HB about her future plans and tells JMM that she is returning to Paris to resume treatment under Manoukhin. Half-heartedly invites him to see her in London on the Sunday prior to her departure. (He does not go.)
28	Orage resigns the editorship of the *New Age*.
30	Goes to Ouspensky's flat in Kensington to obtain a contact address for Gurdjieff.

October

1 (Sun)	Gurdjieff arrives at the Prieuré (Priory) des Basses-Loges at Avon, near Fontainebleau, to found the 'Institute for the Harmonious Development of Man'.
2	With LM leaves England for the last time.
3	Arrives in Paris, taking rooms at the Select Hotel, Place de la Sorbonne (where she stayed during the war as she points out in a subsequent letter to JMM) and noting down the cost of meals for the next few days. Describes the lovely journey to Paris, and Paris itself, in a letter to Brett.

<table>
<tr><td>4</td><td>Has further treatment from Manoukhin who promises KM a complete recovery by Christmas but who quickly writes to Gurdjieff saying that KM must continue with his treatment and is no state, currently, to enter the Priory.</td></tr>
<tr><td>6</td><td>Asks JMM if Tolstoy's diaries are obtainable.</td></tr>
<tr><td>9</td><td>Finishes her work on Koteliansky's translation of Dostoevsky's letters to his wife and posts it to him. She is critical of the Dostoevsky which the letters reveal although reluctantly distinguishing between the letter-writer and the writer of books.</td></tr>
<tr><td>13</td><td>Describes the beauty of autumnal Paris to JMM, says she still cares for DHL and would like to meet him after she has left Paris, but reveals that she is going to see Gurdjieff in Fontainebleau next week.</td></tr>
<tr><td>14</td><td>KM's 34th birthday. A Dr Young, from the Priory, gives her a medical examination. Orage, himself on the way to the Priory, arrives in Paris and visits KM who, in a long notebook entry, admits that since coming to Paris she has felt as ill as ever, cannot work and believes her spirit almost dead. So what has she to lose by going to Gurdjieff? 'Risk! Risk anything! Do the hardest thing on earth for you.'</td></tr>
<tr><td>15</td><td>Urges JMM to grow things, to garden, to come into contact with the earth that way. Sits in the Luxembourg Gardens cold and unhappy.</td></tr>
<tr><td>16</td><td>Young telephones to say that a room is ready.</td></tr>
<tr><td>17</td><td>Travels to Avon with LM who, on 18, returns to Paris to pick up some things for KM, then soon leaves again.</td></tr>
<tr><td>18</td><td>Describes the Priory for JMM and tells him she is 'under observation' for a fortnight.</td></tr>
<tr><td>19</td><td>Informs Koteliansky that she intends to learn to work manually and will revert to writing stories only when she is a better person.</td></tr>
<tr><td>23</td><td>Describes her daily routine to JMM whose account of Jeanne Beauchamp's wedding [earlier in the month] has saddened her.</td></tr>
<tr><td>24</td><td>Tells JMM that she believes only Gurdjieff can help her. She does want to write – but differently.</td></tr>
</table>

| 25 | LM hears from KM that she is staying indefinitely. |
| 27 | Further describes life at the Priory for JMM. |

November

Early this month, after enjoying a sumptuous room at the Priory almost since her arrival, is moved to a small, cold, spartan room which she attempts to endure.

2 (Thurs)	Tells JMM that Gurdjieff is going to build a couch for her in the stable where she can sit and inhale the cows' breath. Later she will be in charge of them.
7	Eliot violently disparages KM in a letter to Pound.
10	By now is learning Russian.
c.11	Much of KM's laundry is stolen. She quickly writes to LM for replacements.
12	Mentions to JMM an oriental dance performed at the Priory that says more for her about a woman's life than any book or poem.
19	Continues to describe life at the Priory which she loves to JMM. In a later letter to him suggests that DHL and Forster are two men who could understand the place.

December

1 (Fri)	Tries to put JMM off from visiting her until the spring.
6	Describes to JMM the cowshed which she visits every day. Must have a photograph of him.
9	Repeats to JMM that she still wants to write but 'different books'. Contemporary literature, except for Hardy, sickens her.
12	Describes her living conditions to LM. It is very cold and she is having to do hard kitchen work. Nevertheless she believes that this life is right for her.
15	Apologizes to Brett for not writing for a month and thanks her for offering to send some good tea.
17	Praises Gurdjieff to JMM: he seems to understand exactly what she needs and, after the recent intense cold, has restored her to her original sumptuous room. Through JMM arranges Christmas presents for Jeanne and Chaddie Beauchamp and him.
22	Tells LM that an old-fashioned English Christmas is being planned for 60 people at the Priory and says much the

	same to JMM on 23. (Later, quite possibly on New Year's Eve, writes another letter to LM with her news, but does not send it.)
26	Thanks JMM for the Rothenstein drawing of him which she likes much more than the photograph which he has sent. She now believes that in life the head should not dominate but be in balance with one's emotional and instinctive sides. Above all, she wants to be real.
31	In a final burst of letter-writing which takes her into the New Year begins, but does not finish, a letter to Chaddie and Jeanne Beauchamp; tries to explain to Elizabeth Beauchamp the physical and mental states which led her to the Priory. She is tired of her old stories 'like birds bred in cages' and will not write any more until the spring. She bids her cousin farewell; to HB mentions affectionately old times and other members of their family and asks JMM to come on 8 or 9 January and stay for about a week so that he can experience the opening of the new theatre on 13.

1923

EVENTS, THE ARTS, LITERATURE: German mark continues its disastrous slide throughout the year; Irish Civil War ends (May); Hitler's beer-hall putsch in Munich fails (Nov.); Yeats wins the Nobel Prize for Literature (Dec.); deaths of Czech writer Jaroslav Hašek (Jan.) and Sarah Bernhardt (March); Bennett publishes *Riceyman Steps*; Conrad, *The Rover*; Aldous Huxley, *Antic Hay*; DHL, *Birds, Beasts and Flowers, Kangaroo* and *The Ladybird*.

January

5 (Fri)	JMM tells KM that he is overjoyed to be visiting her soon. He plans to arrive on 9.
9	Shows JMM around the Priory on his arrival. Late in the evening runs ahead of him up the stairs but suffers a violent haemorrhage and dies shortly afterwards in her room.
12	KM's funeral in Fontainebleau Protestant Church, attended amongst others by JMM, LM, Chaddie and Jeanne Beauchamp and Brett. She is buried in Avon cemetery.

Monetary Equivalents

Selected amounts of money (referred to in the text by *) and their value in 2005. In pre-decimal British currency one shilling = 5p, therefore the 15 July 1918 entry of £6 6s. should be understood as £6.30.

Date	Amount	UK Sterling 2005	US Dollars 2005	Australian Dollars 2005	New Zealand Dollars 2005
1 October 1907	£2	140.95	275.98	344.29	391.85
24 August 1908	£100	6,798.26	13,310.90	16,605.40	18,899.60
June 1912	£10	659.36	1,291.02	1,610.55	1,833.06
6 March 1916	£156	7,046.34	13,796.70	17,211.40	19,589.30
1 February 1917	£35	1,306.32	2,557.77	3,190.82	3,631.65
February 1918	£208	6,748.67	13,213.90	16,484.30	18,761.70
15 July 1918	£6 6s.	204.41	400.23	499.29	568.27
January 1919	£800	24,489.49	47,950.40	59,818.10	68,082.40
August 1919	£300	9,183.56	17,981.40	22,431.80	25,530.90
September 1920	£40	1,070.48	2,096.00	2,614.76	2,976.00
c. 22 May 1921	FR2,000	1,144.44	2,239.95	2,794.34	3,180.39
7 September 1921	£10	295.49	578.60	721.77	821.48
7 September 1921	£12	354.59	694.29	866.12	985.78
1 November 1921	£300	8,864.74	17,357.10	21,653.00	24,644.50
31 January 1922	FR4,500	3,030.41	5,933.54	7,402.09	8,424.74

A Who's Who in the Mansfield Chronology

There is no set pattern in the entries which follow and the length of an entry does not necessarily reflect the importance of that person in Katherine Mansfield's life. Rather they are designed to give substance to the lives of those people who figure in Mansfield's life, and indeed to say more about her own life, in a way that the format of the preceding narrative does not permit. Where it is deemed particularly helpful, there are references to the Chronology and works cited in the Bibliography.

Baker, Ida Constance (LM) (1888–1978) was born in Stuston, Suffolk, the daughter of a colonel. ('Constance', 'daughter' and 'colonel' inevitably call to mind Constantia and 'The Daughters of the Late Colonel'. As Ida Baker herself said in her book, she is gently caricatured in that story.) When she was still a baby the family went to Burma, not returning until she was seven. They then settled in Welbeck Street, London, and Ida and her sister entered Queen's College School (the junior part of Queen's College) as day girls. They moved to Queen's College itself in 1901. Ida's mother died early in 1903 so she became a boarder at the college like KM (nine months her junior) and her sisters who entered the college during the same year. The two girls met immediately and, some months later, KM, rather oddly, proposed friendship. When Ida was studying to become a professional violinist she wanted to take her mother's name, Katherine Moore. But KM wanted 'Katherine' for herself and proposed she take her brother's name, Lesley. Thus 'Lesley Moore', so often shortened to 'L.M.', was born.

From the time they met until KM's death 20 years later, Ida Baker is far and away the most important woman in KM's life. Servant, companion, friend, confidante, wife, she selflessly played whatever role KM wanted her to. During those 20 years there were only three periods of time when she was not either living with her or available at her beck and call: (1) when KM returned to New Zealand, October 1906 to August 1908; (2) when Ida was in Rhodesia for a few months in 1911, her father and brother having settled there the year before and (3) when she was again in Rhodesia, travelling there in late March 1914 and returning in the autumn of 1916. Of course Ida experienced the totality of KM's emotional range during those 20 years, from deep venomous hatred to utter dependence on her. After KM entered Gurdjieff's Institute (Ida's contemporary diary fixes the exact date) she took a job on a farm at Lisieux, near Caen. All too soon she was called to attend KM's funeral.

After KM's death Murry employed Ida to type her manuscripts for £10 a month, a good choice as she was used to KM's execrable handwriting. Ida also worked as a housekeeper for Elizabeth Russell (Beauchamp) in her London home and at a bungalow in Wood-green, a village in the New Forest. There in 1942, with a woman friend she had made, Helen Harvey, she moved into a small cottage. Her companion died the following year but she stayed on and in 1971 finally published *Katherine Mansfield, the Memories of LM*, with a linking commentary by Georgina Joysmith and a foreword by the pioneering American Mansfield scholar, Sylvia Berkman. This book she intended as a vindication of KM who had been, as she saw it, done down, sold short by a wide circle of people both in her life and after her death in memoirs, reminiscences and biographies. She thought KM's father mean towards her and could not forgive Murry for publishing so much of her writing posthumously when she (KM) had expressly ordered the opposite. She also thought that Antony Alpers had got things wrong in his first biography of KM (1953) despite her assisting him in preparing it. Of KM's friends only Koteliansky comes out well in her book.

Beauchamp, Annie Burnell (AB) (1864–1918) was born in Sydney, Australia, to Joseph and Margaret Isabella Dyer (née Mansfield). Shortly after her marriage to Harold Beauchamp in 1884 her mother and two of her sisters, Kitty and Belle, came to live with them. Thus it was that Granny Dyer rather than Annie Beauchamp became the most important adult in the early lives of the children (and the affection she lavished on them is returned in the portrayal of the grandmother figures in the stories). Against Annie Beauchamp's action in cutting KM from her will on her return from Europe in 1909 (Chronology, 13 August 1909) may be balanced KM's tribute to her on hearing of her death (Chronology, 8 August 1918).

Beauchamp, Harold (HB) (1858–1938) was born in Ararat in the State of Victoria, Australia, in November 1858, the eldest surviving child of Arthur and Mary Elizabeth Beauchamp née Stanley (Elizabeth Stanley was a pseudonym KM occasionally used). His father, something of a rolling stone, moved his growing family to Picton on the north-eastern tip of South Island, New Zealand, in 1861 and Harold went to school there. After some years in Wanganui, on North Island, the family moved in 1876 to Wellington and the following year Harold joined the importing firm of W.M. Bannatyne and Co. It is probably not too much to say that he turned the fortunes of the company round, becoming a partner in 1889 and sole partner five years later. In 1884 he had married Annie Burnell Dyer whom he had been courting since she was 14 and who, like him, had been born in Australia. They were years of great success for Harold. In the 1890s he began to gather company directorships such as the Gear Meat Company and the Equitable Building and Investment Company. As detailed in the Chronology, he regularly moved his family to bigger and better properties. In 1898 he became a director of the Bank of New Zealand and its chairman in 1907.

That same year he arranged for a local reporter, Tom Mills, to evaluate KM's work. This led to her publication in the Melbourne periodical, the *Native Companion*, later in the year. Having thus helped to launch her career (and also paying for his three eldest daughters to finish their education in London, 1903–6), he now proceeded to grant her an allowance of £100 p.a. on her return to England in 1908. Over the years this was regularly increased: in 1916 it was £156, in 1919 £260 and by November 1921 £300 p.a. (see the table of Monetary Equivalents). Despite her fears that he might stop her allowance he never did. Nor did he take the (surely reasonable) attitude that once she was married to Middleton Murry, the latter should assume sole responsibility for providing for her. He was similarly generous to his other daughters all of whom, like KM, eventually left for the northern hemisphere.

Meanwhile his wife Annie had died in 1918, leaving him a lonely man. In January 1920 he married Laura Bright, a family friend. After KM's death three years later, he arranged that 47 Fitzherbert Terrace, Wellington, her last address in New Zealand, be donated to the nation and the proceeds used towards the establishment of a National Art Gallery. He was also persuaded to donate £200 to the Alexander Turnbull Library for the purchase of her first editions. In 1929 he was dismayed to learn that her body was not in a proper grave but in the 'fosse commune' at Avon which could be re-used. Without bothering to contact Middleton Murry, for whom he seems to have had little time, he sent Jeanne's husband, Captain Renshaw, to France to sort the matter out.

Later in the year in which KM died Harold Beauchamp was knighted for services to New Zealand finance. In 1937 he published *Reminiscences and Recollections* for private circulation amongst friends. (There is a copy in the British Library.) In his meticulous recording of dates and events (he also carefully notes the increasing tonnage of the ships he and his family travelled on) it is an extremely useful source for Beauchamp family history. He also speculates that the literary bent of the family – he is thinking of Elizabeth as well as KM – is attributable to her grandfather, John (see the Family Tree), the so-called 'Poet of Hornsey Lane'. Harold gave the job of editing and revising the book to his friend Guy Scholefield who also contributes the chapter on KM. Finally, it should be noted that in her two longest works of fiction, 'Prelude' and 'At the Bay', KM portrays her father as 'Stanley Burnell' but assuming an exact equation between fact and fiction would be dangerous.

Beauchamp, Leslie Heron (LB) (1894–1915) was the longed-for son of Harold and Annie Beauchamp, their youngest child. The 'Heron' was a family name (a great-uncle was Henry Herron Beauchamp) but within the family he was known as 'Chummie' or 'Bogey' (the latter was one of KM's names for Murry). Harold and Annie were not going to repeat the experience of sending their younger children to England to complete their education, so Leslie was educated at Waitaki Boys' High School on South Island. He was dutifully preparing to follow his father into business but, after the outbreak of the First World

War, joined the British Army in New Zealand and came to England for training in February 1915. He soon met KM (Chronology, February 1915). After training in various locations around the country he returned to London in August, staying with KM and Murry for a week in Acacia Road and discussing New Zealand with her. As a bombing officer in the South Lancashire Regiment he left for France on 22 September and was killed just over a fortnight later. KM always claimed that in his dying words he mentioned her (Chronology, 19 November 1915) but the latest research suggests that 'Katy' was KM's own addition (see Ferrall and Stafford: *Katherine Mansfield's Men*). He and KM were certainly close, however, and his death left a void for her as it did for her father (see his *Reminiscences and Recollections*). She attempted to fill that void by addressing him directly in her notebook (Chronology, 22 January 1916) and feeling spurred on to write about the New Zealand they both remembered. Certainly her best work all dates from after Leslie's death and her mother also remarked on her (KM's) reconciliation with the rest of her family following his death (Chronology, 16 March 1916).

KM and Murry called the dream house that they were going to live in after the war 'The Heron' in memory of Leslie. It never came about. However, quite apart from the totality of her best work, her stories 'Six Years After' and 'The Fly' and her poem 'To L.H.B (1894–1915)' directly resulted from his death.

Beauchamp, Mary Annette (1866–1941), known as **Elizabeth** and famous for her book *Elizabeth and her German Garden,* was a daughter of Henry Heron Beauchamp, an uncle of Harold Beauchamp's (see the Family Tree). She was born in Sydney, Australia, in 1866 and in 1890 married Count Henning von Arnim, 15 years her senior. He is the 'Man of Wrath' in *Elizabeth and her German Garden* (published anonymously in 1898 and still popular over 100 years later) in which she describes the garden she created and lovingly developed on her husband's estate at Nassenheide in Pomerania. Both Forster and Hugh Walpole tutored her children there. After her husband's death in 1910 she moved to Switzerland and build the 'Chalet Soleil' near Randogne-sur-Sierre below Montana. One visitor there was John Francis, the 2nd Earl Russell (Bertrand Russell's elder brother) whom she married in 1916. The marriage proved unhappy and was dissolved after little more than three years. One result of that was her fine novel *Vera,* depicting life with the 2nd Earl.

All told she had published 22 books by the end of her life. KM reviewed two of them in the *Athenaeum*. They had met a few times prior to 1921 but when the Murrys moved to Chalet des Sapins in Montana in the middle of that year KM and Elizabeth were within half-an-hour's walk of each other. Each wary of the other at first, they met frequently and a warm friendship began to develop. They were proud of each other's achievements. KM wrote affectionate letters to her, including one of the last she ever wrote, on 31 December 1922. Not having received this, Elizabeth wrote to her on 3 January to say how much she missed her. Two books on Elizabeth, by Leslie de Charms and Karen Usborne, are cited in the Bibliography.

Belloc-Lowndes, Marie (1868–1947) has a walk-on role in the life of KM. Of part French ancestry, the sister of Hilaire Belloc, she was a novelist. She and KM met, thanks to Edward Marsh, towards the end of February 1921 and the two corresponded a little during the next three months. She gains her place for the key letter KM wrote to her on 26 May 1921, the relevant part of which is worth quoting here in full:

> ... Illness is a great deal more mysterious than doctors imagine. I simply can't afford to die with one very half-and-half little book and one bad one and a few --- ? stories to my name. In spite of everything, in spite of all one knows and has felt – one has this longing to *praise Life* – to sing ones minute song of praise, and it doesn't seem to matter whether its listened to or no. Will one ever be able to say how marvellously beautiful it all is? I long, above everything, to write about *family love* – the love between growing children, and the love of a mother for her son, and the father's feeling – But warm, vivid, intimate – not 'made up' – not *self conscious.*

Bibesco, Princess Elizabeth (1897–1945) was the daughter of Herbert Asquith, Liberal Prime Minister 1908–1916, and Margot Asquith. In 1919 she married Prince Antoine Bibesco who was First Secretary at the Romanian Legation in London before the First World War. The 'philandering' (Murry's word) with him developed in the autumn of

1920 when he was in Hampstead and KM at the Villa Isola Bella, Menton. Rather tactlessly, about the beginning of December, he sent KM a story by Bibesco which she refused to read and returned to him (Murry published it in the *Athenaeum*, 14 January 1921). To Murry himself KM put on a brave face about the relationship between him and Bibesco but recorded her misery in her notebook. It may have led at least partially to her abandoning reviewing for the *Athenaeum* (Chronology, 8 December 1920). She was further depressed by his long letter to her of c.10 December confessing his relationship with other women, particularly Bibesco. The latter, not prepared to let matters rest, wrote to him in March 1921 when he had returned to KM in Menton. KM saw this letter and wrote sadly to Ida Baker about it and magisterially to Bibesco herself (Chronology, 20 and 24 March 1921). Bibesco published her short stories *I Have Only Myself to Blame* in 1921 and *Balloons* in 1922.

Bowden, George (1877–1975), the son of a Baptist minister, won a choral scholarship to Kings College, Cambridge, 1899–1902, his years overlapping Forster's there. Later he taught singing and elocution and sang at small concerts. Ida Baker suggests that it was through Margaret Wishart, a friend of KM's at Beauchamp Lodge, that KM met him, although she puts the meeting back to autumn 1908 (Chronology, February 1908). Why KM wanted to marry in such haste – *he* was plainly in love with *her* – is open to speculation but her pregnancy by Garnet Trowell (if she *was* pregnant by then) presumably had something to do with it. She also probably wanted the protection and respectability that a wedding ring and a married name conferred on her and certainly used Bowden's name as her surname whilst alone on the continent in 1909. On her return she summoned Bowden from Easton Hall, Lincolnshire, where he was attending a house party, and suggested they live together. Ever sympathetic and accommodating, Bowden invited her to his flat in Gloucester Road, Marylebone, and there she stayed probably until she had her operation towards the end of March 1910. It was during this time that Bowden was instrumental in bringing about the all-important meeting between KM and Orage (for these events see the Chronology).

Bowden always insisted that the impetus for divorce came from him. So it was that when he wished to remarry divorce proceedings were begun in October 1917. As recorded, as soon as the decree became absolute in May 1918 KM and Murry married. Bowden also married. He lived some 20 years in the U.S. pursuing a successful career in public speaking.

When Antony Alpers was preparing his first life of KM (*Katherine Mansfield, a Biography*, New York, 1953) he approached Bowden for an account of his relationship with her. This he carefully wrote in a long series of letters copies of which can be seen in the Alexander Turnbull Library, Wellington.

Brett, Dorothy (1883–1977), 'Brett' to her friends, the daughter of the second Viscount Esher with whom she had a difficult relationship, was a painter. She studied at the Slade School of Art from 1910 to 1916 and by 1915, the year in which she met KM, had a studio off the Earls Court Road. She was drawn into Ottoline Morrell's Garsington circle and became friends with, amongst others, Mark Gertler, Murry, Beatrice Campbell and Virginia Woolf. She had a lively and kind personality so it is not difficult to see why many people were attracted to her. She and KM may have had a particular reason, however, for the friendship that developed rapidly between them in 1916: both regarded themselves as outsiders. Brett was profoundly deaf and felt intellectually outclassed. KM was a 'colonial'. In September 1916 both had flats at 3 Gower Street. KM moved out at the beginning of February 1917; Brett stayed for a total of nine months.

During the years that followed the two kept in touch – there are about 100 extant letters from KM to Brett – but the former was deeply upset when she learnt in August 1920 of the intimacy between Brett and her husband that had developed that year. Nevertheless she felt able to forgive her and the friendship resumed. Her last finished story, 'The Canary', was a present for Brett (Chronology, 7 July 1922) to whom she wrote on New Year's Eve that year in a final flood of letter-writing. Twelve days later Brett attended her funeral.

KM once predicted that Brett and Murry would marry after her death. They were close in 1923 but the following year Brett accompanied D.H. Lawrence and Frieda to New Mexico where she made her home for the rest of her life, dying in Taos in 1977. In 1933 she published a memoir of her relations with Lawrence (*Lawrence and Brett: a Friendship*, reissued with an Epilogue in 1974) and there is a biography of her by Sean Hignett, *Brett* (1984).

Campbell, Beatrice and **Gordon**. KM met Gordon Campbell (1885–1963) late in 1911. An Irishman, he was a barrister at the Inns of Court at that time and became Assistant Controller at the Ministry of Munitions during the First World War. Later he was Director of the Bank of Ireland. He succeeded his father as Lord Glenavy. In 1912 he had married Beatrice (1885–1970) who was born in Dublin and went to Dublin Metropolitan School of Art and then the Slade.

Beatrice's friendship with KM dates from 1912. In the late summer or early autumn of 1913 KM and Murry stayed with the Campbells in their cottage at Howth just to the north of Dublin and the following February, when he had to leave KM in Paris to attend a Bankruptcy Court hearing in London, Murry lodged with the Campbells in South Kensington. Thereafter, however, they seem to have changed their opinion about Gordon, although remaining close to Beatrice. KM stayed with the Campbells for a few days in July 1916 and something of the old friendship between the four of them appears to have been recaptured at the successful Christmas party the Murrys gave in 1918.

As KM was increasingly abroad during her last years she and Beatrice saw much less of each other, although the friendship remained. An account of it is given in Beatrice's autobiography *Today We Will Only Gossip* (Bibliography C, under 'Glenavy').

Cannan, Gilbert (1884–1955), a prolific novelist, married Mary, the ex-wife of J.M. Barrie, in 1910. The Cannans became very friendly with KM and Murry in the years leading to the First World War. Gilbert contributed to *Rhythm* (and later to the *Blue Review*) and was one of those writers who helped to keep the periodical alive in 1912. He was also responsible for the nickname 'the Two Tigers' for KM and Murry (which became 'Tig' and 'Wig' in their letters to each other).

In the spring of 1913 the Cannans persuaded them to move to a cottage in Cholesbury, Buckinghamshire, near their own converted windmill where they stayed (Murry just at weekends) until the beginning of July. The Cannans also hosted the notorious 1914 Christmas party in which, in a playlet devised by Murry, KM refused to conform to the script.

After that the Cannans dropped out of the lives of KM and Murry. KM was sharply critical of two of Gilbert's novels which she reviewed in the *Athenaeum* in 1919. By then he had suffered a nervous break-down and his marriage had failed. He finally descended into madness and published nothing in the last decades of his life.

Carco, Francis (1886–1958) was born François Carcopino-Tusoli in Nouméa, the capital of the French Pacific island of New Caledonia (only about 1,000 miles from New Zealand). His family was Corsican. He arrived in Paris in 1910 and Murry met him there during his Christmas vacation of 1910–11, soon signing him up as a foreign cor-respondent for *Rhythm*. He wrote poetry and fiction and established himself as a chronicler of artistic and bohemian life in Paris.

The Chronology records his first meeting KM (May 1912). Her cor-respondence with him became increasingly passionate at a time when she was feeling dissatisfied with Murry and led to his inviting her to Gray (Chronology, January 1915) where he was serving in the French army not as a fighting soldier but as a postman for a baking unit. As recorded, her journey there was fictionalized in 'An Indiscreet Journey'. Murry seems to have taken the affair remarkably calmly. Perhaps he realized that Carco was filling a temporary need in KM's life which would come to nothing. If so, he was absolutely right for, although KM made use of Carco's Paris flat in March and May 1915, she resolutely refused to go to Gray again, declaring to Murry 'F[rancis] C[arco]... simply doesn't exist for me' (letter, 9 May 1915).

Both Carco and KM made use of their affair in fiction. In *Les Innocents* (1916) Carco portrays KM as the Englishwoman Winnie Campbell and himself as 'le Milord'. It is a violent novel ending in the deaths of both Winnie and le Milord. In 'Je ne parle pas français', written by KM partly as a response to *Les Innocents* in about ten days (January/February 1918) and her third longest story after 'Prelude' and 'At the Bay', Carco is portrayed as the callous Raoul Duquette and Murry as the weak, selfish Dick Harmon. In one of her most powerful portrayals of the isolated, vulnerable woman KM herself is Mouse.

In later life, after novels such as *Jésus-la-Caille* (1914), *L'Équipe* (1919) and *L'Homme Troqué* (1922), for which he won a French Academy award, Carco published a number of books of memoirs in which he mentions KM. In his *Bohème d'Artiste* (1940) he calls her an Australian. Carco died in Paris in 1958.

Carrington, Dora (1893–1932) was a painter. KM met her in 1915 and their friendship developed at Garsington weekends during 1916. Towards the end of that year Carrington, like Brett (with whom she had become friends when they were at the Slade), had a flat in the same house as KM and Murry, 3 Gower Street. She had the top-floor flat, KM and Murry were on the ground floor and Brett in the middle. KM, however, felt spied upon by the tenants of the other flats and was relieved to be able to move out after only four months or so. At the Garsington Christmas during that period KM allotted the part of Muriel Dash to Carrington in her hilarious playlet 'The Laurels'. Carrington herself loved KM's own ambiguous dressing-up, the role-playing and the games.

Carrington was loved by Mark Gertler but, although she married Ralph Partridge in 1921 (as KM remarked in a letter to Brett), was herself devoted to Lytton Strachey of whom she painted a well-known portrait in 1918. She committed suicide shortly after Strachey's death in 1932.

De la Mare, Walter (1873–1956) became known to KM and Murry as a contributor to *Rhythm*. Although never particularly close to them, something they probably both regretted – see Murry's letter to KM of 19 April 1920 – they liked and respected him. In her formal will of 14 August 1922 KM asked that one book in her possession be given to De la Mare.

De la Mare was a poet who wrote many volumes of poetry for adults (e.g. *The Listeners and Other Poems*, 1912) and children (e.g. *Peacock Pie*, 1913). His collection *The Fleeting and Other Poems* includes the poem 'To K.M.'. He was also a novelist (*Henry Brocken*, 1904; *The Return*, 1910; *Memoirs of a Midget*, 1921), short story writer, essayist, critic and anthologist. He was particularly good at evoking the uncanny and supernatural. He is unjustly neglected today.

Drey, Anne Estelle (1879–1959) was born Anne Estelle Rice into a large Irish-American family living near Philadelphia. She worked first as a magazine illustrator in the U.S. but took up painting seriously after arriving in Paris in 1906 where she established herself as a mural painter and book illustrator. It was there that she met KM in 1912. They became and remained close friends until the latter's death. It was there too that she met her future husband,

O. Raymond Drey, a journalist, art and drama critic, whom she married in 1913. She contributed regularly to *Rhythm*. Staying in Cornwall in 1918, she booked KM into the Headland Hotel, Looe, in May of that year and began the famous portrait of her in a bright red dress a month later. After her marriage London became her base for the rest of her life.

Fergusson, John Duncan (1874–1961), a Scottish painter, met Murry in 1910 in Paris and introduced him to his fellow Fauvist Anne Estelle Rice (as she then was). A painting of his called 'Rhythm' gave Murry the title for the magazine he co-founded in the summer of 1911. Fergusson met KM in May 1912 and they quickly became good friends. By 1917, living nearby, Fergusson regularly dined with KM and Murry at Redcliffe Road and he was one of the people to whom she vividly described her frightening journey to Bandol in January 1918. A few months later, with Brett, he witnessed the Murrys' wedding. The Woolfs so hated the woodcut design he did for the front cover of their edition of 'Prelude' that only a few copies were printed making use of it; the rest were plain. He lived for some time with the choreographer Margaret Morris who wrote a book on him with the honest title *The Art of J.D. Fergusson, a Biased Biography* (Bibliography C).

Gaudier-Brzeska, Henri (1891–1915), a Frenchman, had a brief but violent relationship with KM and Murry. A brilliant, but impoverished, modernist sculptor who contributed drawings to *Rhythm*, he met KM in the summer of 1912. Later that year there was a plan that his companion Sophie Brzeska (who had persuaded him to add her name to his) would live with the Murrys in their cottage in Runcton with Gaudier joining them at weekends. However, he accidentally overheard KM criticizing her and that effectively ended that possibility. As a result of the incident he wrote an incoherent letter to Murry attacking KM. He attacked Murry himself physically about six months later when he stormed into his office with the woman cartoonist George Banks demanding payment (which had not been promised) and snatching two drawings from the wall (Chronology, 12 May 1913).

After the outbreak of war Gaudier-Brzeska joined the French army and was killed on 5 June 1915. For further information on him and his relationship with KM and Murry see H.S. Ede's *Savage Messiah* and Murry's own autobiography *Between Two Worlds*. In that book Murry compares Gaudier-Brzeska temperamentally with Lawrence, a point KM biographers have developed.

Gerhardie, William Alexander (1895–1977) was born in St Petersburg of English parentage, went to school in Russia and joined the Scots Greys during the First World War because the Tsar was colonel-in-chief. He also served in the British Embassy in Petrograd (as St Petersburg was then called) and was awarded the OBE for his services with the British military mission in Siberia 1919–20. He then went to Worcester College, Oxford.

It was there that his correspondence with KM, whom he never met, began. He attended Murry's lectures on style (Chronology, May 1921) and shortly afterwards, having read one of the stories written by KM to which he (Murry) had made passing reference, wrote to her about it. This was 'The Daughters of the Late Colonel'. As the Chronology relates (23 June 1921), KM replied from Sierre, obviously delighted that someone had understood a most misunderstood story. Some months later Gerhardie asked if he might send her his first novel, *Futility*, which other writers had disdained. She not only agreed, but read the novel quickly and sent him a detailed critique of it (Chronology, 12 November 1921). Her kindness did not end there for she offered to write to Richard Cobden-Sanderson recommending that he publish the book. Thus it was that, overhauled in a way suggested by KM, *Futility* was published by Cobden-Sanderson in 1922. KM's letter to Gerhardie of 21 November 1921, in which she lists some of the 'unfashionable things' she likes, is particularly attractive.

Gerhardie published several later novels such as *The Polyglots* (1925) and *Of Mortal Love* (1936). He also wrote *Anton Chehov* (sic) (1923), *The Romanovs* (1940) and an autobiography, *Memoirs of a Polyglot* (1931). KM wrote to 'Mr Gerhardi'. The final 'e' of his surname did not put in an appearance until 1967.

Gertler, Mark (1892–1939). Like the poet and fellow artist Isaac Rosenberg (1890–1918), Mark Gertler came from a poor East-End Jewish family originating in Eastern Europe and studied at the Slade School of Art. Their lives, however, developed very differently. Gertler was good-looking, good company, a witty conversationalist and, soon after leaving the Slade, regarded as an artist of great promise. He was a protégé of Gilbert Cannan (and later of Edward Marsh) who portrayed his early life in his novel *Mendel* (1916). More importantly, Cannan introduced him to Ottoline Morrell's pacifist Garsinton set. By the middle of the war (which killed Rosenberg) he had made it as an artist. For years he loved Carrington but she eventually abandoned him for Lytton Strachey.

Gertler met KM in 1914. Immediately after the Cannans' Christmas party of that year he was remorseful about the role he had played, as he described in a letter to Strachey. His and KM's paths crossed occasionally during the next few years. He was with her when she publicly defended Lawrence's *Amores* at the Café Royal (Chronology, 30 August 1916). Their friendship, however, cooled after the war. In a letter to Murry of 10 October 1920 KM unforgivingly recalls his callous behaviour towards her when he heard that she had tuberculosis. Now, however, as she notes, he is ill. He committed suicide in 1939 when his tuberculosis was already advanced.

Goodyear, Frederick (1887–1917), whose father was a prosperous coal merchant, met Murry while they were both at Brasenose College, Oxford. Murry said he was a brilliant undergraduate. He had a gift for nonsense and parody and wrote songs and poetry. More practically he wrote the manifesto for the first number of *Rhythm* in the summer of 1911. Some months later Murry met KM and quickly introduced her to Goodyear, the first of his friends to be so introduced, as Murry himself noted. They became close friends and Goodyear accompanied the others on their visit to Paris, December 1913 to February 1914. During the war he served first as a corporal in the Meteorological Office of the Royal Engineers but, bored with that and wanting to see action, accepted a commission with the Essex Regiment. He was then given leave and visited KM and Murry at Mylor, Cornwall, in July 1916. He seemed fatalistic about his chances and that probably contributed to the depression KM was feeling by the second half of August. In May the following year, during the battle of Arras, he was badly wounded and died a few days later. In 1920 his father published *Frederick Goodyear, Letters and Remains 1887–1917* with a memoir by F.W. Leith-Ross.

Goodyear's death, which she linked with Chummie's, shook KM. She did not normally keep letters which she received (except for

Murry's), but she kept his. Similarly, she reserved the teasingly affectionate name of 'Betsy' for both men. In a surviving draft of one letter from her to him in the *Collected Letters* (4 March 1916) she warns him off – in a letter to her he had hinted that things would have been very different between them had Murry not been around – yet writes the sort of letter which is designed to delight him.

Gurdjieff, George Ivanovich (or George Georgiades) (1866–1949) was born in Aleksandropol (now Gyumri in present-day Armenia) to a Greek father and Armenian mother. His passport gave 1877 as the year of his birth and other sources suggest 1872, but 1866 is probably more likely. Very little is known about his early life and then only from his own account, but, just before the First World War, he had established a group of followers in Moscow. In the aftermath of the Russian Revolution he led some of these followers to T'bilis (Tiflis in present-day Georgia), where he founded the Institute for the Harmonious Development of Man, thence to Constantinople, Berlin and Paris. He finally settled in the latter city where he acquired the Prieuré des Basses-Loges at Avon (near Fontainebleau, 40 miles south of Paris), once a Carmelite monastery, and opened it, as the Chronology relates, little over a fortnight before KM's arrival.

With her reading of *Cosmic Anatomy*, discussions with Orage and attending lectures by Ouspensky, KM was clearly attempting some sort of spiritual solution after all the physical cures then available had failed her. Obviously she was in no fit shape to do the hard physical work (such as digging trenches) that was part of the regime, but she did help in the kitchen and attend the elaborate movement and dance exercises on which Gurdjieff's Institution placed so much emphasis. Although her constant refrain was 'It is intensely cold' she never criticized Gurdjieff and he seems to have treated her with great kindness and consideration.

In 1924 Gurdjieff was involved in a bad car crash – he was an appalling driver – and the Institute was never the same after that. In 1932 the Priory closed its doors and was sold the following year. Gurdjieff went back to Paris and spent the rest of his life there, except for a few visits to America, usually pretty incomprehensibly writing up his teachings. After his death in 1949 his body was taken back to Avon where he was buried only a few yards from KM's grave.

Mystic, charlatan, guru, egomaniac, crook, con man, Gurdjieff has been called all of these things and probably was all of them. Much has been written about him and Bibliography C cites some of these works. James Moore is a particularly lively and by no means wholly sceptical commentator.

Hastings, Beatrice (1879–1943) was born Emily Alice Haigh in South Africa. In the early years, 1910–11, of KM's association with the *New Age*, edited by A.R. Orage, Hastings was Orage's mistress, and from July to the late summer of 1910 KM stayed with them in Kensington. At first all was well between the two women who had much in common (neither was English, both were separated but not divorced from their husbands). Hastings, a formidable, passionate and malicious journalist, had much to teach the younger woman. At the end of February 1912 after visiting Geneva, KM was staying with the others in Sussex but by then she had met Murry and her association with *Rhythm* had begun. Hastings and Orage jealously saw it as a dangerous rival to *New Age* and quickly began attacking it in their own publication, singling out KM's work for particularly savage criticism (Chronology, March 1912–January 1913). This clearly marked the temporary end of relations between KM and Hastings.

In 1914 Hastings left Orage and by 1915 was in Paris, moving amongst artists and writers and becoming the lover of the Italian painter Amedeo Modigliani (1884–1920) who conferred immortality of a kind on her in paintings and drawings. In March 1915, when KM was staying at Carco's Paris flat, the two women met at a party. According to KM's own account (letter to Murry, 22 March) Hastings appears to have become drunk and quarrelled furiously with her. That marked the permanent end of their relationship.

Hastings's accounts of Paris in wartime appeared in *New Age*; her last contribution was published on 10 August 1916. Later, perhaps true to form, she began to hate Orage, whereas KM began publishing in *New Age* again in 1917 and was reconciled to him. Hastings seems never to have been able to accept KM's success as an imaginative writer, hysterically attacking her in pamphlets as late as the 1930s. Her last years were fuelled by depression and drink. In October 1943 she offered her MSS to the British Museum for safe keeping. After receiving an official refusal she gassed herself.

Huxley, Aldous Leonard (1894–1963) was from a famous family. T.H. Huxley was his grandfather, Matthew Arnold a great-uncle and his elder brother Julian became a distinguished biologist. During the First World War he was a member of the Garsington set not so much because of pacifism (although books he published in the 1930s such as *Eyeless in Gaza* and *Ends and Means* adopted a pacifist position) but because his bad eyesight exempted him from military service. KM met him during those years and he visited her in London, although they were not especially close.

In January 1919 Murry became editor of the *Athenaeum,* appointing Sullivan as his assistant editor and Huxley as the second assistant editor. KM was unhappy with the latter appointment calling Huxley in a letter to Murry (7 January 1920) 'very silly and young sometimes – and watery headed'. When Huxley's book of short stories, *Limbo,* was published in 1920 KM felt unable to review it for the *Athenaeum,* dismissing it as 'BILGE'. Conversely and fair-mindedly, she praised his review of Edward Thomas's *Collected Poems* when it was published later the same year.

'Bliss' and 'Marriage à la Mode' are said to contain satiric portraits of a Huxley-type character. He himself satirized Garsington and its people, Bertrand Russell, KM, Murry, Ottoline Morrell herself, in a series of Peacockian novels published in the twenties (*Crome Yellow, Those Barren Leaves, Point Counter Point).* In the next decades novels, short stories, verse, historical studies, travel books and essays continued to pour from his pen although he is famous today for perhaps just one book, his dystopian *Brave New World* (1932). Having set the opening of one of his novels on the day of Gandhi's assassination, he managed to die on the day of John F. Kennedy's assassination.

Koteliansky, Samuel Solomonovitch (1882–1955), a Ukrainian Jew, studied at the University of Kiev and came to England in 1911. Loving the country and fearing the attentions of the Tsarist secret police if he returned home, he stayed for the rest of his life. He first worked for the Russian Law Bureau in High Holborn, living above the office and translating Russian legal documents. When KM and Murry left 5 Acacia Road in November 1915 the house was taken by a Russian journalist, Michael Farbman and his wife Sonia. 'Kot' (as he was known to his friends) rented a room from them. Later he owned the house and lived there until his death. He resigned from his job in 1917 and thereafter lived precariously as a reader for the Cresset Press and freelance translator. Passionately fond of literature, he worked on translations of Chekhov, Dostoevsky, Tolstoy and others with (besides KM) Gilbert Cannan, Lawrence and the Woolfs, producing all told more than 30 works of translation. In the spring of 1923 Murry became editor of a new monthly, the *Adelphi*, and for a time Kot worked with him. However, by the end of the following year the two had fallen out over the periodical and this was one breach in Kot's life which was never repaired. In 1929 he became a naturalized British subject. A prey to black moods and depression, he was shaken by the death of Lawrence the following year and by Gertler's suicide in 1939. On his own death in 1955 he bequeathed to the British Museum ten volumes of letters from correspondents such as KM, Cannan, Gertler and Ottoline Morrell. He left to the British Museum no less than 346 letters from Lawrence.

Kot met Lawrence in the summer of 1914 and the latter lost little time in introducing him to KM and Murry. As Geraldine Conroy's article makes clear (Bibliography D), Kot and KM could have met each other as early as August 1914. He was one of the group at the Christmas 1914 parties when he sang his favourite Hebrew song which gave Lawrence the name 'Rananim' for the utopian colony of like-minded souls living apart from the world (over a century before Coleridge had had a similarly crackpot idea). The friendship between Kot and KM flourished over the next 20 months. He was with her when the Café Royal incident occurred (Chronology, 30 August 1916). However, there was little or no contact between them during the next two years. Perhaps Kot, an emotional and generous man, felt his friendship was being taken for granted and it was not until KM invited him to Portland Villas in September 1918 that the breach was healed.

Kot must be credited with introducing KM to many Russian authors. During the last four years of her writing life they collaborated on about six works of translation from the Russian. The most important of these is their translation of Chekhov's letters (Chronology, April–October 1919). They also worked on Gorki's *Reminiscences of Leonid Andreyev* (Chronology, September 1922) and *Dostoevsky: Letters and Reminiscences* 'translated from the Russian by S.S. Koteliansky and J. Middleton Murry'. This was published in 1923 after KM's death. No acknowledgement of her assistance in the translation is made but she in fact helped him in the way she assisted him in their other collaborations, i.e. by putting his halting translation into good English. Another collaboration, confirmed by Kot, was the second story, 'Captain Ribnikov', of Alexander Kuprin's *The River of Life and Other Stories* (1916).

There was another breach between the two during 1920. There were no letters from KM to Kot between December 1919 and February 1921 when she writes him a conciliatory letter asking his forgiveness. In October of that year she again attempts a reconciliation and asks for further information about Dr Manoukhin – which he provides. Manoukhin's treatment did her no good, but it at least brought KM and Kot together again in the last two years of her life. He was denied permission to attend her funeral.

Lawrence, David Herbert (DHL) (1885–1930). By the time KM wrote to Lawrence requesting a contribution to *Rhythm* he was already an established writer with such books as *The White Peacock* and *The Trespasser* behind him. The four, KM and Murry, Lawrence and Frieda, first met in June 1913. The Chronology records the fluctuating relationships between the two couples over the next five years: professional, uneasy, close, sometimes too close as when KM and Murry were unwilling witnesses of the violence between the Lawrences in the spring of 1916 at Higher Tregerthen, Cornwall. (It was Lawrence's insistence that they join them there that put an end to the happiest time KM and Murry spent together: Bandol, January to March 1916.) In October 1918 Lawrence sent her his feeble play *Touch and Go,* but there is no clear evidence that she recognized herself in the sculptress Anabel Wrath.

In April 1919 Lawrence was furious with Murry's offhand dismissal of some of the contributions he had submitted to the *Athenaeum* and his venom extended to KM. Nevertheless she continued to think of him and write perceptively about him in her letters. She thought little of his novels *Women in Love* (1921) and *The Lost Girl* (1920) but *Aaron's Rod* (1922) renewed her admiration for the writer. She was also pleased, in September of that year, to receive his postcard from Wellington.

In February 1923, about three weeks after KM's death, Lawrence wrote emotionally about her to Murry and a year later violently attacked the Gurdjieff Institute as a sham in a letter to Mabel Dodge Luhan. In his short story 'Smile' (*The Woman Who Rode Away and Other Stories*, 1928) Lawrence returns to the attack on Murry, depicting him, as he views his wife's body in a convent, as a weak, vacillating man. Lawrence himself succumbed to tuberculosis in 1930, aged 44. There is a whole library of books on him. The latest, excellent biography is by John Worthen (Bibliography C).

Lawrence, Frieda (FL) (1879–1956), born Frieda von Richthofen, had married Ernest Weekley, many years her senior, in 1898. They had three children, Montagu, Barbara and Elsa. Lawrence met Frieda when he lunched with Weekley, by then Professor of French at the University College, Nottingham, at the latter's home. This was in early April 1912. A month later the two had eloped to the continent. They married in July 1914. See Tedlock (Bibliography C) and Frieda Lawrence's *Not I, But the Wind...*

Marsh (Sir) Edward Howard (1872–1953) was a life-long and successful civil servant. In 1912 he was Winston Churchill's Private Secretary at the Admiralty. But he was also a generous patron of the arts and that same year met KM and Murry through Rupert Brooke (whose *Collected Poems,* with a long memoir, he issued in 1918) and published the first of his influential anthologies of *Georgian Poetry* which Lawrence enthusiastically reviewed in *Rhythm* the following year. When *Rhythm* ran into financial difficulties towards the end of 1912, after Granville had absconded, Marsh it was who guaranteed Murry's overdraft, thus greatly assisting the continued existence of *Rhythm* for a few more issues.

During the war he supported the painter Mark Gertler and in 1916 helped Murry to obtain an interview for a post at the Home Office (Murry was unsuccessful). His anthologies continued to appear – there were five all told between 1912 and 1922 – but their quality began to decline and Murry launched an attack on the falsity of *Georgian Poetry, 1918–1919* in the pages of the *Athenaeum* (Chronology, 5 December 1919) which helped to pave the way for the triumph of Eliot and the modernists in the 1920s. Marsh was hurt by the attack. In 1921, however, he was instrumental in KM and Marie Belloc-Lowndes becoming acquainted, a meeting KM warmly thanked him for. Marsh published his reminiscences, *A Number of*

People, in 1939 and Bibliography C cites Christopher Hassall's biography.

Morrell, (Lady) Ottoline Violet Anne (OM) (1873–1938) was the daughter of Lieutenant-General Arthur Cavendish-Bentinck and his second wife, Lady Bolsover. She was the half-sister of the sixth Duke of Portland (hence her title). In 1902 she married Philip Edward Morrell (1870–1943) who was a Liberal M.P. from 1906 to 1918, first for South Oxfordshire and from 1910 for Burnley.

From 1908 she began to attract a wide circle of intellectual, literary, artistic and political celebrities at her Thursday night gatherings in her Bloomsbury home, 44 Bedford Square. Her role as a patroness of the arts became even more extensive and famous when, in 1915, she and her husband bought Garsington, an Elizabethan manor six miles from Oxford. Most of the literary and artistic colleagues of KM and Murry who figure in the Chronology in the years immediately before, during and immediately after the First World War, and many more besides who do not, like Henry James, W.B. Yeats and George Santayana, visited Ottoline Morrell's Bloomsbury home or Garsington or both. The atmosphere at Garsington was permissive for its time and, during the First World War, pacifist. Philip Morrell was one of the few leaders of opinion who bravely spoke out against the war.

Ottoline first met Lawrence about the time the war broke out and, by the end of 1915, she had met KM and Murry who, as related, both paid frequent visits to Garsington over the next few years. She was perfectly capable of recognizing talent herself and was immensely kind and generous to her wide circle of friends. For example, when she heard of KM's mother's death, she sent her 'a most exquisite bouquet of bright flowers' (KM to Chaddie Beauchamp, 17 August 1918). But her thoughtfulness was sometimes misunderstood and, tall, striking, dressing eccentrically and possessing an extraordinary voice, she was a larger than life figure. Inevitably she became a target for satire at the hands of her literary friends. *Women in Love*, which Lawrence wrote as a sequel to *The Rainbow* (1915), portrayed her as Hermione Roddice. Circulating in manuscript before publication, it caused the Morrells such deep offence that Philip warned Lawrence's literary agent, the ubiquitous J.B. Pinker (who ultimately also became KM's literary agent), that he would sue the publisher should the work appear. This put an end not only to the friendship between Ottoline and Lawrence but also to any prospect for its immediate publication which was delayed until 1920 (and then only a limited American edition for subscribers) and 1921 (first British edition).

Similarly, Ottoline was depicted as Priscilla Wimbush in Aldous Huxley's first novel, *Crome Yellow* (1921) and this too caused offence and the break-up of a friendship. Perhaps rather surprisingly, Huxley returned to the attack in *Those Barren Leaves* (1925) whose Mrs Aldwinkle is at least partially based on Ottoline. Her memoirs, edited by Robert Gathorne-Hardy (Bibliography C), were published long after her death which took place at Easter 1938.

Murry, John Middleton (JMM) (1889–1957) was ten months younger than KM. He was born in Peckham, south London, to John and Emily Murry, lower middle-class parents who were ambitious for their son (his brother did not arrive for another 13 years). Murry won a scholarship to Christ's Hospital School which he entered in January 1901. It was then in Newgate Street, near St Paul's Cathedral, but the following year moved its premises to Horsham in Sussex. In 1908 he went to Brasenose College, Oxford and, while still an undergraduate, founded with Michael Sadleir the periodical *Rhythm* through which he met KM a few months later. From early 1912 to her death in 1923, their lives were completely entwined. When they were not together they were writing to each other. C.A. Hankin (Bibliography C) publishes or lists some 400 letters from Murry to KM, a figure only dwarfed by her letters to him (about half as many again in the first four volumes of the *Collected Letters*).

After her death Murry set about publishing a huge amount of Mansfieldiana. His initial vehicle for this was a new literary periodical, the *Adelphi,* of which he was the editor and the first number of which appeared in June 1923. For a year no number went by without containing something by KM. But he was also intent on publishing her remaining fiction, *The Doves' Nest and Other Stories,* which included 15 unfinished stories in 1923, *Something Childish and Other Stories* in 1924 and *The Aloe* (her first version of 'Prelude') in 1930. Her *Poems* was published in 1923, her *Journal* in 1927 and her *Letters,* in two volumes, in 1928. Her book reviews for the *Athenaeum* were published as *Novels and Novelists* in 1930, her *Scrapbook* (thus mistakenly giving the impression that she kept a) a journal and b) a scrapbook) in 1937 and her letters to Murry himself in 1951. Finally, there was the so-called 'Definitive Edition' of her *Journal,* which was not definitive, in 1954. Murry's editions of her poems, journal, 'Scrapbook' and all her letters have been superseded by later editions (see Bibliography A and B).

Murry's devotion to the memory of KM did not end there. He wrote about her (see Bibliography C), introduced and selected new editions of her stories (for example, an American edition of *In a German Pension* in 1926), wrote an introductory note to Ruth Elvish Mantz's *Critical Bibliography* (itself superseded by B.J. Kirkpatrick's monumental work, Bibliography A) and co-operated with Mantz in bringing out a biography of KM in 1933. In the posthumous reputation of KM there are two separate issues here which the reader can pursue in the biographical and critical studies: (1) to what extent was he carrying out KM's wishes regarding her unpublished material, to what extent flouting them? (2) Was he making her reputation or milking it? Plainly one's view of his character is relevant here.

Whatever else one may think of Murry one must admire his industry. In addition to all the editorial and critical work already mentioned, he published numerous books. Although he had no gift for imaginative work (pace KM) – his novel *Still Life* was still-born – he published *Dostoevsky* in 1916, *The Problem of Style* (his 1921 Oxford lectures) in 1922, *Keats and Shakespeare* in 1925 and, controversially, *Son of Woman, the Story of D.H. Lawrence* in 1931. George Lilley (Bibliography C) lists his entire output.

After KM's death Murry seriously considered marrying Brett but actually, in April 1924, married a young woman of Huguenot stock, Violet le Maistre. She had first come to his attention by sending stories to the *Adelphi,* one of which he published. If this has echoes of KM submitting material to the editor of *Rhythm,* the parallels go much further. Violet looked like KM and deliberately modelled herself on her in her dress, hairstyle and mannerisms. She even died, in her early thirties, of tuberculosis. Unlike KM however, she was able to give Murry children. Katherine Middleton Murry, whom they called Weg (more echoes) was born in 1925 and John Middleton Murry Junior, Colin or 'Col', in 1926. In the last year of Violet's life Betty Cockbayne had been employed by Murry to help in the house. Now, to the dismay of his friends, he proceeded to marry her. She may have been an excellent housekeeper and cook, but the marriage proved disastrously unhappy. They had two children. Mary born in 1932 and David in 1938, but ultimately he walked out of the relationship. By then he had met Mary Gamble whose interest in left-wing politics, the Peace Pledge Union of the 1930s and 1940s and Christianity mirrored his own contemporaneous interests. She became his fourth wife as soon as Betty died in 1954. By then he was living at Lodge Farm Thelnetham, in Suffolk, where he attempted to develop in practice the concept of an ideal community (which harks back to Lawrence). Although he continued to work and publish until nearly the end – he died on 13 March 1957 and is buried in Thelnetham churchyard – the causes which he espoused in the last 25 years or so of his life had become unfashionable and his criticism, in an age of increasing specialization, dated. Bibliography C cites both his autobiography, *Between Two Worlds* (1935), which concludes in 1918 but still has much on KM, and the biography by his friend F.A. Lea (1959).

Murry is a controversial figure in the life of KM. At the very least his detractors regard him as weak and taking the line of least resistance. They ask why he was not with her more often when she was lonely and sick and her letters were shouting out for his company. Why, when they were together, did he invariably choose the best room for his study and seem to put his interests before hers? Why did he not make more effort to be pleasant to her father when the two men met in August 1919? (Thenceforward Harold Beauchamp appears to have treated him with contempt.) Why, when she was already dying, did he choose to have affairs with Brett and Elizabeth Bibesco? Why, at the very end of her life, pushed out of her room by the medical staff, did he not force his way back in like Henry at the end of Hemingway's *A Farewell to Arms*? Why did he not ensure that KM's body should be buried in a proper grave at Avon, not the 'fosse commune'?

Against these sorts of charges answers can be made. KM was a brilliant letter-writer changing chameleon-like according to her recipient, but she was manipulative, working on his (or her) emotions and never more so than when writing to Murry. His own health was decidedly poor at times, he suffered from pleurisy and collapsed from overwork. Furthermore, he had to earn a living and took that imperative seriously. He did not come from a wealthy family as KM did. Through him she met many of the literary and artistic greats of the day. If he had affairs, succumbing to temptation after years of looking after a sick and demanding wife, so did she – with Carco (whom she met through him). He seems to have suffered from a genuinely bad memory. This may explain the 'fosse commune' at Avon. Why, after KM's death, did he publish so much that incriminated him when he could so easily have destroyed it? Ultimately perhaps he did make her reputation, as well as create her myth. The jury is still out on the KM/JMM relationship and will be reconvened *sine die*.

Murry, Richard (1902–1984) was born **Arthur** but KM disliked that, preferring to call him Richard, the name he finally adopted. Murry's younger brother first met KM in the spring of 1912 at his parents' house in Nicosia Road, Wandsworth Common, before Murry joined KM at Clovelly Mansions. Richard contracted tuberculosis but recovered and, thanks to his brother, worked as a farmhand at Garsington to aid his recovery. The two brothers established the Heron Press in the basement of Portland Villas and Richard developed an interest in book production. They published Murry's *Poems 1917–18* (dated 1918, but printed between December 1918 and June 1919) and then, in an edition set, printed and bound by Richard, KM's own 'Je ne parle pas français' (officially published February 1920). In 1919 he was working for the publisher Richard Cobden-Sanderson but, encouraged by the artists in the KM/Murry circle such as Brett to believe in his artistic talent, decided to try for the Slade School of Art. Early in 1921 he received news that he had been awarded a London County Council Scholarship for the Slade.

KM's relations with Richard were friendly, even playful and relatively uncomplicated. Her letters to him reveal a genuine concern for his welfare. She regarded him as something of a lucky mascot as he had had tuberculosis and beaten the disease. Moreover, some of the huge affection she had for her younger brother was transferred to him, Murry's younger brother, on Leslie's tragic death. On KM's own death he attended her funeral in Avon and designed the lettering for her stone as he did for his brother's tombstone over thirty years later.

Newland-Pedley, F. (1854–1944) is one of the minor saints in the story of KM. An FRCS, he specialized in dentistry and co-founded the dental school at Guy's Hospital, London, in 1889. In December

1915, after Murry returned to London, KM stayed on at the Hotel Beau Rivage in Bandol, feeling lonely, ill and depressed. Her rheumatism was particularly troublesome. It is now that Newland-Pedley makes his brief appearance in her narrative (Chronology, 14 December 1915). In a series of letters to Murry she describes how the Englishman first of all lends her copies of the *Times* – that in itself cheers her – then suggests a cure for her rheumatism, an ointment which he proceeds to obtain for her. Furthermore it works. From being totally unable to walk on 13 December, on Christmas Day she is going on the sort of long and difficult walk, including climbing, he has stayed on at the hotel specifically to show her. Throughout she emphasized his shyness and old-fashioned courtesy.

Murry took up Newland-Pedley's story in *Katherine Mansfield and Other Literary Portraits* (Bibliography C): in 1930, a sick and old man, he arrived at the village of Aquaseria, near Como, Italy, seeking accommodation at an inn. He was so impressed by the way the proprietors looked after him, and saw him through to a complete recovery, that he decided to remain for the rest of his life in the village. His subsequent kindness to the villagers, particularly the children, became, as Murry says, almost legendary. Finally, he refused to admit that Italy and England might be at war and, according to Murry, both the Italian and German authorities let him go his own way. He died in the village aged 90 and his generosity in funding the building of the church is commemorated in a plaque there. In his will he left £900 in annuities to be paid yearly to five Italians and the residue, some £60,000, to Guy's.

Orage, Alfred Richard (1873–1934) was born in Yorkshire and at an early age took up school- mastering. He moved in theosophical circles and joined the I.L.P. and the Fabian Society. In 1895 he married Jessie Dwight, a cousin of Dwight Eisenhower, but the couple were divorced in 1904. Two years later he went to London and in 1907, partly financed by G.B. Shaw, began to edit *New Age* with the principle of not paying contributors, who dubbed it 'No wage'. Even so, established writers and newcomers, all appeared in the pages of the magazine – Shaw himself, Bennett, Wells, Pound, T.E. Hulme, Herbert Read, Chesterton, Belloc, Edwin Muir and many others – including KM.

Orage is unusual in KM's life in that he weaves his way in and out of it, rather than knowing her for her whole life or for a given part of it. The Chronology relates that he was the first to publish her stories in England (in 1910); how, drawn to Murry and *Rhythm,* she deserted *New Age,* Orage and his mistress Hastings; how in their fury, they counter-attacked (Chronology, March 1912–January 1913; also Hastings in the 'Who's Who...'). That might have been it, and for some years was it, but in 1917 Orage is publishing her again in his magazine (Chronology, April–December). He disappears from her life again only to reappear in 1921 when, seemingly out of the blue, KM gushingly writes to him thanking him for all that he has taught her (Chronology, 9 February 1921).

This letter led to a renewal of their friendship. When KM came to London in August 1922 the two met. They discussed Ouspensky and Gurdjieff and Orage may have attended one or more of the former's lectures with KM. They both decided, but for different reasons, to join Gurdjieff's Institute at Avon and Orage duly resigned the editorship of *New Age.*

Orage found exhausting the physical work, digging, to which he was assigned at the Priory. He would return to his cell (sic) literally crying with fatigue. However, Gurdjieff seems to have judged his man and, shortly after he (Orage) felt he had reached rock bottom, told him he had dug enough and changed the medicine. In fact he did more than that. He sent Orage, after little more than a year at Avon, to New York where he duly spread the word.

Orage stayed some seven years in America. Back in England in 1931, as active as ever, he founded *New English Weekly* the following year and edited it until his death which occurred suddenly on 6 November 1934 just after he had made a BBC broadcast. For more about Orage see Bibliography C (Philip Mairet and Wallace Martin).

Orton, William Aylott (1889–1952). If his autobiographical novel *The Last Romantic* (1937) is to be believed – and he insisted to Alpers that he had faked nothing – then Orton helps to fill in one or two gaps in the obscure narrative of KM from her return to England in August 1908 to her meeting Murry at the end of 1911. Orton, or 'Michael' as he calls himself in his novel, met KM at a Hampstead tennis party probably in the late summer of 1910. He was a young schoolmaster tortured by his love for another woman ('Lais' in the novel). In KM he seems to have found a woman of his own age, of similar interests in literature and music and a similar ambition to be a writer, who could provide in a platonic friendship a refuge from the agonies of his passion. The *Collected Letters* reproduces from *The Last Romantic* two letters from KM to Orton (there is no other source). Similarly, Murry's 1954 edition of the *Journal* reproduces diary entries made by the KM character 'Catherine' in the novel.

In September 1911 Orton renewed his friendship with her after her return from Bruges and Geneva but the relationship – 'affair' would probably imply too much – ended with a letter she wrote to him just after Easter 1912 (wrongly dated 15 April 1911 in Vol. I of the *Collected Letters*). Ida Baker in her *Memories* suggests that KM's poem 'There Was a Child Once' (which appeared in *Rhythm* on 13 March 1913) sums up their relationship which may also have contributed to the dreamy, unreal atmosphere of 'Something Childish But Very Natural' written by KM at the beginning of 1914.

Orton contributed to *Rhythm* and years later to the *Athenaeum*. On the outbreak of war he joined up and survived the Gallipoli disaster of 1915. He also served in Egypt and France. From 1917–19 he worked with the intelligence staff at the War Office and was in the industrial relations department of the Ministry of Labour for the next three years. From 1922 until his death he was on the staff of Smith College, Northampton, Massachusetts, specializing in economics and publishing books and articles on a wide variety of subjects.

Ouspensky, Piotr Demianovich (1895–1947) is a vital link, with Orage, between the KM living in Sierre during the summer of 1922 and the KM who entered Gurdjieff's Institute in the autumn. As a young man Ouspensky was a mathematician and journalist. He also read in the occult and, about 1905, drafted a novel which was not published in Russia until 1915 and not in English translation (as *Strange Life of Ivan Osokin*) until shortly before his death in 1947. He first met Gurdjieff in Russia during the First World War and seems to have had an on-off relationship with him over the next few years. However, having met with Gurdjieff again in Constantinople in 1920 and having published in the same year *Tertium Organum,* which expounded his system, he arrived in London in August 1921 to prepare the way for Gurdjieff.

Ouspensky was an immediate hit in some intellectual circles in the capital. KM probably heard about him through Orage, and Murry believed that the real reason why she decided to visit London so suddenly was not so much to consult Dr Sorapure as to find out more about Ouspensky and Gurdjieff. Murry himself trailed along unwillingly, hating all that Ouspensky stood for (another profound sceptic was Lawrence). In the event, although KM did attend one lecture of Ouspensky's (and possibly more) and met him personally, Gurdjieff despite his support was denied residency in the U.K. and so drew some of Ouspensky's followers away from London to France, to the Institute at Avon. Ouspensky himself visited KM there about the end of October and confirmed the medical view that she was dying.

About a year after KM's death Ouspensky broke his formal links with Gurdjieff and abandoned his whole system shortly before his own death. His book *In Search of the Miraculous*, published posthumously in 1950 in London, is a record of his years as Gurdjieff's pupil.

Russell, Bertrand Arthur William (1872–1970), later 3rd Earl Russell, figured briefly in the story of KM. They first met, through Lawrence, in the summer of 1915 and their paths may well have crossed during the following summer at Garsington, but it was from November 1916 until February 1917 that their friendship was at its closest with their dining together, visits – they were both at Garsington for Christmas 1916 – and intimate letters. Russell denied, however, that they ever had an affair while admitting that the letters might imply otherwise. Their friendship seems to have ended after KM told him how shocked she was by his cynical conclusion to an article in the series 'The World After the War'. It has been suggested that KM's 'Psychology', first published in *Bliss and Other Stories*, is an exploration of her relations with Russell – and also with Ida Baker.

Russell lived a long and tumultuous life. From 1895 he was a Fellow of Trinity College, Cambridge. During the First World War he worked for conscientious objectors and was sent to Brixton Prison (where he read, and disliked, 'Prelude') for, according to the authorities, prejudicing relations with the U.S. in an article he wrote. In the 1960s he was active first in the Campaign for Nuclear Disarmament and then on the Committee of 100 and went to prison for his anti-nuclear protests. He was married four times and had numerous affairs. He succeeded his brother (who was briefly unhappily married to 'Elizabeth', KM's second cousin) as the 3rd Earl Russell.

He was a prolific author writing many books on mathematics – which he tried to show was reducible to logic – academic and popular philosophy, such as the monumental *History of Western Philosophy*, society and education. He won the Nobel Prize for Literature in 1950. The Bibliography, C, cites the biography by Ronald Clark and the second volume, covering the years 1914–44, of his autobiography.

Sadleir, Michael (1888–1957) was born Sadler but changed his name to Sadleir to distinguish himself from his father, Professor Michael Sadler. He went to Oxford (Balliol) and whilst there met Murry. The two men founded *Rhythm* in 1911, financed by Professor Sadler who generously contributed £50. His son's involvement did not last long, however, after KM's arrival on the scene. KM and Sadleir were never close. She may have regarded him as too much of a bourgeois. He had a brief diplomatic career and then joined the publishing firm of Constable in which he rose from publishing editor to director (1920) and finally managing director. KM and Murry first thought of Grant Richards as the publisher of *Bliss and Other Stories* but Sadleir approached them and, quickly accepting Murry's terms, became the publisher – not before he had insisted on some cuts, however, which KM agreed to reluctantly and later bitterly regretted (Chronology, April and December 1920). She refused point blank to have *In a German Pension* re-issued by Constable but the firm did publish *The Garden Party and Other Stories* in 1922.

Sadleir was an expert bibliographer who compiled a huge collection of nineteenth century fiction which formed the basis for his classic two-volume *Nineteenth Century Fiction: A Bibliographical Record* (1951). He also did bibliographical and editorial work on Anthony Trollope. His love of the Victorian period and knowledge of London are reflected in what is by far his best-known novel, *Fanny by Gaslight* (1940).

Schiff, Sydney (1868–1944) came from a wealthy, artistic family. His grandfather had been a successful banker and his father founded the firm of A.G. Schiff and Co. Initially Schiff went to Canada to farm but felt that that was not his true vocation and returned to England about 1910 to write. His first marriage had failed but then he met and fell in love with Violet Beddington (1876–1962), one of several daughters (another was Ada Leverson, the novelist and friend of Wilde who called her 'The Sphinx') of an extremely musical family. The Schiffs married in 1911 and divided their time between the Villa Violet, at Roquebrune, and London. Over the years they patronized the arts and cultivated many literary and artistic friendships with, for example, Eliot, the Sitwells, Proust – the last volume of whose *A la recherche du temps perdu, Le temps retrouvé,* Schiff translated on the death of C.K. Scott Moncrieff – Aldous Huxley and Max Beerbohm. Schiff published novels under the name of Stephen Hudson (KM reviewed *Richard Kurt* in the *Athenaeum,* Chronology, 7 November 1919) and financed the illustrated quarterly *Art and Letters* which published two stories by KM ('The Pictures' and 'The Man Without a Temperament', Chronology, Autumn 1919 and Spring 1920). Not the least of Schiff's achievements was to organize the famous party at the Majestic, Paris, attended by Diaghilev, Stravinsky, Proust and Joyce. Seven weeks earlier he had also been instrumental in the meeting between Joyce, KM and Murry.

According to Virginia Woolf, the relationship between KM and Schiff did not start well: Schiff approached her about contributing to *Art and Letters* and daringly offered her some advice to which she took umbrage, savagely cutting him down to size in her reply (the letter has not survived). The Schiffs were not the sort of people to bear grudges, however, and when Grant Richards alerted her, in Menton, to their presence in nearby Roquebrune and she wrote to them, they immediately responded and a firm friendship quickly developed (Chronology, April 1920). Over the next few years they saw each other and frequently corresponded, but their last meeting of all, in London on 17 September 1922, was spoilt by the offensiveness of another artist whom the Schiffs had cultivated, Wyndham Lewis.

Sobieniowski, Floryan (1881–1964), a Pole, was educated at Cracow University and then studied art history and aesthetics in Munich and Paris between 1909 and 1911. He was a drama critic in Cracow 1911–12 and contributed to *Rhythm* as its Polish correspondent. He met Shaw in 1912 and translated more than 40 of Shaw's plays into Polish (he also translated Galsworthy). Living in London 1913–29 he also pestered Shaw for money. The playwright eventually told him to return to Poland and stay there. After KM's death Murry tried to help him, on two separate occasions, by supporting his application for a grant from the Royal Literary Fund. He did finally return to Poland where he died in 1964.

At best Sobieniowski can be seen as someone who admittedly scrounged off KM (and Murry) – for example at Runcton in 1912 – but who nevertheless developed her interest in Slavic literature, possibly even introducing her to the work of Chekhov and certainly to that of the Pole Stanislaw Wyspianski whom he encouraged her to translate and about whom she wrote a poem (Chronology, 26 December 1910).

At worst Sobieniowski is an unprincipled scoundrel, a Rasputin (KM's word). It is he, it is suggested, who infected her with gonorrhoea when they were lovers in Bavaria in 1909 from which so many of her later medical problems arose (Chronology, March 1910). Furthermore, although when she was travelling back to England at the end of 1909 she managed to avoid him, in later years he plagued her and this behaviour culminated in his blackmailing her in 1920. He demanded £40 for the return of some letters she had written him when they first knew each other. The theory is that the letters acknowledge in some way that KM's 'The Child-Who-Was-Tired' was a direct plagiarism of Chekhov's 'Spat Khochetsya' (1888) and this explains not only KM's desperation to obtain the letters and have them destroyed, but also her point blank refusal to allow *In a German Pension*, which included the story, to be republished. It is stressed that hard evidence is lacking for the main allegations against Sobieniowski in this paragraph.

Sorapure, Victor Edgar (1874–1933) was KM's favourite doctor, the one she invariably returned to from the time she was first introduced to him by Anne Drey in September 1918, when he was a consultant at Hampstead General Hospital, to the time she finally left England four years later. He it was who first clearly explained to her the gonococcal origin of her arthritis, or what she habitually referred to as her 'rheumatiz'. He it was who advised her to go south in the winter and, understanding her and realizing the crucial link between her will to live and her ability to write, advised her not to enter a sanatorium (where writing would be forbidden). He was the first doctor whom she felt she could talk to freely, and their discussions plainly ranged beyond the physical. She originally dedicated 'The Daughters of the Late Colonel' to him, wrote an amusing poem in limericks which begins with him and, alone of all her many doctors, left him a book in her will.

In a letter to Anne Drey (13 January 1919) KM volunteers the information that Sorapure was a foundling left on a Paris doorstep with the name SORAPURE pinned on his chest. He was educated at St George's Jesuit College, Kingston, Jamaica and, after taking his medical degree and doing postgraduate work in Scotland, returned to Kingston as chief surgeon at Government Hospital. He then became a Professor of Clinical Medicine at Fordham University (New York) 1906–10. Both there and when he was a general practitioner and consultant in London during and after the First World War he was greatly respected by both patients and colleagues. He himself died of tuberculosis before the age of 60.

Strachey, (Giles) Lytton (1880–1932), the biographer and essayist, was central to the Bloomsbury group and a frequent visitor to Garsington. After a miserable childhood and year at Liverpool College, he went to Trinity College, Cambridge, which mentally liberated him. He was a member of the Apostles there. During the war he made no secret of his pacifism. In 1918 he published *Eminent Victorians* which was an immediate success and the iconoclasm of which meant that the Victorian age from then on was viewed in an entirely different light. He followed this success with another masterpiece, *Queen Victoria* (1921), which was similarly irreverent but shot through with a grudging, even affectionate respect for the monarch. In the last years he formed a ménage à trois with Ralph Partridge and Dora Carrington.

Although KM allotted him one of only six parts in her Boxing Day 1916 playlet 'The Laurels', Strachey does not figure largely in her life. They first met in November 1915. She plainly intrigued him and his *Letters* (edited by Paul Levy) reveal that he thought it would probably be worthwhile to dig behind the mask of her face. He once wrote to her praising her reviews in the *Athenaeum* (Chronology, 3 October 1919) to which he also contributed.

Sullivan, John William Navin (1886–1937), an Irishman, married Vere (Evelyn) Bartrick-Baker, a friend of KM's from her Queen's College days, during the war. He was a versatile writer, producing books of popular science, *Beethoven: His Spiritual Development* (1927) and an autobiographical novel, *But for the Grace of God* (1932).

He became friendly with Murry – Sullivan was always much more a friend of Murry's than KM's – after reading his *Dostoevsky: A Critical Study* (1916). The two were colleagues during 1917 at the War Office and early in 1919 Murry appointed him as an assistant editor of the *Athenaeum* with Aldous Huxley, who admired his intelligence and liveliness, as the second assistant editor. KM's own attitude to him fluctuated a good deal as can be seen by the references to him in her letters. 'He is a good chap', she writes on 22 February 1918, but four months later she finds him 'a coward and utterly abominably selfish'. She found his presence at the Villa Isola Bella (March/April 1921) something of a strain and clearly viewed his contributions to the *Athenaeum* with a critical eye. He may well have been the first to proclaim KM a 'genius' in print (*Athenaeum*, 2 April 1920, Chronology) but Lawrence for one found such puffing of Murry's wife's work in his periodical a bit rich.

Swinnerton, Frank (1884–1982) left school at an early age and worked his way up: office boy, proof reader and finally editor at Chatto and Windus. He published many novels, perhaps the best-known of which is *Nocturne* (1917). (KM was decidedly lukewarm about a later novel, *September* (1919), in the *Athenaeum*.) Swinnerton was also a freelance journalist, drama critic and publisher's reader. All this literary and journalistic activity meant that he was a well-known figure amongst his fellow writers in the first half of the twentieth century and indeed beyond – he was President of the Royal Literary Fund 1962–6 and his book on Bennett appeared in the 1970s. He was similarly well placed to review the contemporary literary scene which he did in such works as *A London Bookman* (1928) and *Figures in the Foreground* (1963). Both of these books mention KM as does *Swinnerton: An Autobiography* (1937). A second volume of autobiography was *Reflections from a Village* (1969).

Swinnerton became a friend of KM's as a contributor to *Rhythm*. He was one of several writers, Wells was another, who supported the periodical in its financial difficulties in 1912. Years later he contributed to the *Athenaeum* and attended the party which KM and Murry threw at Portland Villas soon after its launch. His portraits of her in his critical and autobiographical books are noticeably perceptive and affectionate. He mentions a last, accidental meeting with her in a restaurant, but alas gives no details.

Trowell, Garnet Carrington (1888–1947). Garnet, a violinist, and his brother Thomas (q.v.), a cellist, first met KM in 1902. They came from an artistic, middle-class family whose father, born in Birmingham in 1858, had emigrated in 1880 to New Zealand where he married and settled. Thanks to local patronage (Chronology, 1902), including that of Harold Beauchamp, the boys, both promising musicians, were able to study in Europe. They left New Zealand in June 1903 (six months after KM) and studied for a year at the Hoch Conservatorium, Frankfurt, before proceeding to the Brussels Conservatorium. By 1907 they were established in London where their parents joined them. Garnet toured England and Scotland with the Moody-Manners Opera Company in 1908–9, playing in the orchestra under the name of Carrington Trowell. He continued to earn his living as a violinist in orchestras for several years before travelling to South Africa in 1923 where he married a fellow musician, Maria Smith. In 1929 they moved, with their two sons, to her native Windsor, Ontario. In the 1930s he taught the violin, then, during the Second World War, worked for the Ford Motor Company. He died of cancer in 1947.

It was in 1908 that KM, having finally given up on Thomas, fell in love with Garnet, a quieter, more responsive character. Their affair was a passionate one as her letters to him written in the last months of that year reveal. The Chronology details what is known about their relationship in 1908–9, but there is much that is not known or merely speculation. What is certain is that by the middle of 1909 KM had married and left Bowden, her mother had arrived, taken her to the continent and left her there, and Garnet was no longer replying to her letters. She was the vulnerable 'femme seule' she so brilliantly writes about in her stories.

Trowell, Thomas Wilberforce (1888–1966), Garnet's twin brother, was a brilliant cellist who professionally used the name Arnold Trowell. KM was infatuated with him for several years after their first meeting in 1902 but, although he dedicated his *Six Morceaux pour Violincelle*, Op. 51, 1908, to his 'dear friend Kathleen M. Beauchamp', there is little evidence that he had strong feelings for her. (For further details of his family and early life see Trowell, Garnet.)

In Brussels Thomas won the Concours Prize for the cello and in London in 1907 gave some concerts at the Bechstein Hall. Ida Baker faithfully sent KM clippings of his London triumphs but she also informed her that he had transferred his affections to a former Queen's College friend of hers, Gwen Rouse, which gave rise to a rather resigned entry in her (KM's) notebook. Years later Thomas became Professor of the Cello at the Guildhall of Music. From 1937 he was on the staff of the Royal College of Music. He composed concertos for his instrument as well as other orchestral works and some chamber music.

Waterlow, Sydney (1878–1944) was a distant relation of KM's. His grandfather, Henry Herron Beauchamp, and KM's grandfather, Arthur Beauchamp, were brothers (see the Family Tree). He went to Eton and Trinity College, Cambridge, and then entered the diplomatic service. He resigned from the Foreign Office but returned to it during the First World War and was able to pull diplomatic strings in April 1918 to secure KM and Ida Baker's escape back to England from Paris.

Besides being a diplomat, Waterlow was also a scholar and writer who contributed to both the *Blue Review* and the *Athenaeum*. He had once courted Virginia Woolf (who however found him boring) and acted as an intermediary as KM and Murry were becoming acquainted with the Woolfs and Bloomsbury. From October 1919 to April 1920, while KM was at Ospedaletti and then Menton, Waterlow stayed intermittently with Murry at Portland Villas (Murry also stayed at his house in Wiltshire). This arrangement suited Murry very well: he was company and paid Murry rent. KM herself did not seem to mind but certainly did not want Waterlow's wife to establish herself there and wanted Waterlow himself out by the time she returned. Murry acceded to this demand although Waterlow was there again the following autumn after she had gone back to the continent.

KM was rather two-faced about her relative. She wrote him friendly, even fulsome letters but criticized him behind his back, particularly to Murry to whom she said that she distrusted Waterlow and regarded him as her enemy. Almost certainly this is an unfair assessment.

Woolf, (Adeline) Virginia (VW) (1882–1941) was the daughter of Leslie Stephen and Julia Duckworth. She had a sister, Vanessa (who married the art critic Clive Bell) and two brothers, Thoby and Adrian. When their father died in 1904 the family moved to 46 Gordon Square, Bloomsbury, thus forming the nucleus of the Bloomsbury group which years later played an important role in the artistic and intellectual life of the United Kingdom and which included Strachey, Forster, the economist J.M. Keynes and others. In 1912 Virginia married Leonard Woolf. Since her mother's death in 1895 she had suffered occasional mental breakdowns which recurred as she was writing her first novel, *The Voyage Out*. Partly as therapy for her the Woolfs founded the Hogarth Press in 1917 with the policy of publishing new and experimental works. KM's 'Prelude' was their second publication. *Night and Day* (1919) was Virginia Woolf's second novel. KM was obliquely critical of it in the *Athenaeum* and it may be in part because of this criticism, and the literary conversations the two had together, that Virginia Woolf went on to write a series of brilliant modernist novels: *Jacob's Room* (1922), *Mrs Dalloway* (1925), *To the Lighthouse* (1927) and *The Waves* (1931). Amongst several other books *A Room of One's Own* (1929) is an important feminist document. In 1941, at the darkest time of the Second World War and following a severe mental breakdown, she drowned herself in the river near her Sussex home. Her *Diaries* and *Letters,* which she wrote indefatigably, were published after her death (Bibliography C under Anne Olivier Bell and Nigel Nicolson).

The exact date when Virginia Woolf and KM first met is not known, but some time in November 1916 is most likely. During the next year they became close not only because of the forthcoming publication of 'Prelude' but also because they discovered a shared passion for writing. They learnt from each other. But they were also rivals, at times warily circling each other yet keeping out of direct contact. KM was jealous of Virginia Woolf but only because she was able to concentrate on her writing in a settled atmosphere of marital harmony. Virginia Woolf made some snide remarks about KM in her diaries and letters, but also wrote in her diary a week after KM's death: 'I was jealous of her writing – the only writing I have ever been jealous of'. In the same entry she also stated, with deep understanding of both of them: 'I think I never gave her credit for all her physical suffering and the effect it must have had in embittering her.'

Bibliography

The indispensable sources for a Katherine Mansfield chronology are given in Section A below. B comprises other editions of Katherine Mansfield's letters, journals, stories, etc., published after her death; C other books consulted; D articles consulted. E lists plays and works of fiction in which either she is central (as in Janice Kulyk Keefer's *Thieves* and C.K. Stead's *Mansfield*) or a character is said to be based on her. In *Point Counter Point* by Aldous Huxley, Murry is viciously satirized as Burlap sentimentalizing over his dead wife Susan.

A.

Alpers, Antony, *The Life of Katherine Mansfield* (London: Jonathan Cape, 1980).

Kirkpatrick, B.J., *A Bibliography of Katherine Mansfield* (Oxford: Clarendon, 1989).

Meyers, Jeffrey, *Katherine Mansfield, a Biography* (London: Hamish Hamilton, 1978).

O'Sullivan, Vincent and Scott, Margaret (eds), *The Collected Letters of Katherine Mansfield*, 4 vols (Oxford: Clarendon, 1984–1996).

Scott, Margaret (ed.), *The Katherine Mansfield Notebooks*, 2 vols (NZ: Lincoln University Press and Daphne Brasell Associates, 1997).

Tomalin, Claire, *Katherine Mansfield, A Secret Life* (London: Viking, 1987).

B.

Alpers, Antony (ed.), *The Stories of Katherine Mansfield* (Auckland: Oxford University Press, 1984).

Drummond, David (ed.), *Katherine Mansfield, Dramatic Sketches* (Palmerston North, New Zealand: Nagare Press, 1988).

Gordon, Ian A. (ed.), *Undiscovered Country, The New Zealand Stories of Katherine Mansfield* (London: Longman, 1974).

Gordon, Ian A. (ed.), *The Urewera Notebook* (Oxford: Oxford University Press, 1978).

Hankin, Cherry A. (ed.), *Letters between Katherine Mansfield and John Middleton Murry* (London: Virago, 1988).

Hanson, Clare (ed.), *The Critical Writings of Katherine Mansfield* (London: Macmillan, 1987).

McNeish, Helen (ed.), *Passionate Pilgrimage, a love affair in letters* (London: Michael Joseph, 1976).

Murry, John Middleton (ed.), *Journal of Katherine Mansfield* (New York: Knopf, 1927); 'Definitive Edition' (London: Constable, 1954).

Murry, John Middleton (ed.), *Katherine Mansfield's Letters to John Middleton Murry 1913–1922)* (London: Constable, 1951).

Murry, John Middleton (ed.), *The Letters of Katherine Mansfield*, 2 vols (London: Constable, 1928).

Murry, John Middleton (ed.), *Novels and Novelists by Katherine Mansfield* (London: Constable, 1930).

Murry, John Middleton (ed.), *The Scrapbook of Katherine Mansfield* (London: Constable, 1937).

O'Sullivan, Vincent (ed.), *The Aloe with Prelude by Katherine Mansfield* (Wellington: Port Nicholson Press, 1982).

O'Sullivan, Vincent (ed.), *Katherine Mansfield, New Zealand Stories* (Auckland: Oxford University Press, 1997).

O'Sullivan, Vincent (ed.), *Katherine Mansfield, Selected Letters* (Oxford: Clarendon, 1989).

O'Sullivan, Vincent (ed.), *Poems of Katherine Mansfield* (Auckland: Oxford University Press, 1988).

Stead, C.K. (ed.), *Letters and Journals of Katherine Mansfield* (London: Allen Lane, 1977).

C.

Les Amis du Prieuré des Basses-Loges (eds), *Gurdjieff à Avon* (Association Historique d'Avon, 2004).

Banks, Joanne Trautmann (ed.), *Congenial Spirits, The Selected Letters of Virginia Woolf* (London: Hogarth Press, 1989).

Beauchamp, Sir Harold, *Reminiscences and Recollections* (New Plymouth, New Zealand: Thomas Avery, 1937).

Bell, Anne Olivier (ed.), *The Diary of Virginia Woolf* Vol. I 1915–1919 (London: Hogarth Press, 1977); Vol. II 1920–1924 (London: Hogarth Press, 1978).

Bennett, Andrew, *Katherine Mansfield* (Tavistock: Northcote House in association with the British Council, 2004).

Berkman, Sylvia, *Katherine Mansfield, A Critical Study* (London: Geoffrey Cumberlege, 1952).

Bishop, Edward, *A Virginia Woolf Chronology* (Basingstoke: Macmillan, 1989).

Boddy, Gillian (ed.), *Katherine Mansfield, A 'Do You Remember' Life* (Wellington: Victoria University Press and Katherine Mansfield Birthplace Society, 1996).

Boddy, Gillian, *Katherine Mansfield, The Woman and the Writer* (Harmondsworth: Penguin, 1988).

Boulton, James T. (general ed.), *The Letters of D.H. Lawrence*, 7 vols. (Cambridge: Cambridge University Press, 1979–1993).

Brophy, Brigid, *Don't Never Forget* (London: Jonathan Cape, 1966).

Burgan, Mary, *Illness, Gender and Writing* (London: John Hopkins Press, 1994).

Caffin, Elizabeth, *Introducing Katherine Mansfield* (Auckland: Longman Paul, 1982).

Carrington, Dora, *Letters and Extracts from Her Diaries*, ed. David Garnett (London: Jonathan Cape, 1970).

Carrington, Noel (ed.), *Mark Gertler, Selected Letters* (London: Rupert Hart-Davis, 1965).

Carswell, John, *Lives and Letters: A.R. Orage, Beatrice Hastings, Katherine Mansfield, John Middleton Murry, S.S. Koteliansky, 1906–1957* (London: Faber, 1978).

Carter, Angela, *Nothing Sacred, Selected Writings* (London: Virago, 1982).

Cather, Willa, *Not Under Forty* (New York: Knopf, 1922).

Charms, Leslie de, *Elizabeth of the German Garden* (London: Heinemann, 1958).

Clark, Ronald W., *The Life of Bertrand Russell* (London: Jonathan Cape and Weidenfeld & Nicolson, 1975).

Clarke, Isobel C., *Katherine Mansfield, A Biography* (Wellington: Beltane Book Bureau, 1944).

Crone, Nora, *A Portrait of Katherine Mansfield* (Ilfracombe: Arthur H. Stockwell, 1985).

Curtis, Vanessa, *Virginia Woolf's Women* (Stroud: Sutton Publishing, 2003).

Daly, Saralyn R., *Katherine Mansfield* (New York: Twayne, 1994).

Darroch, Sandra Jobson, *Ottoline, The Life of Lady Ottoline Morrell* (London: Chatto and Windus, 1976).

Davies, Dido, *William Gerhardie, a Biography* (Oxford: Oxford University Press, 1990).

Delaney, Paul, *D.H. Lawrence's Nightmare* (Hassocks: Harvester Press, 1979).

Dunbar, Pamela, *Radical Mansfield, Double Discourse in Katherine Mansfield's Short Stories* (Basingstoke: Macmillan, 1997).

Ede, H.S., *Savage Messiah* (London: Heinemann, 1931).

Eliot, Valerie (ed.), *The Letters of T.S. Eliot, Volume I 1898–1922* (London: Faber, 1988).

Farr, Diana, *Gilbert Cannan* (London: Chatto and Windus, 1978).

Ferrall, Charles and Stafford, Jane (eds), *Katherine Mansfield's Men* (Wellington: Katherine Mansfield Birthplace Society in association with Steele Roberts, 2004).

Fullbrook, Kate, *Katherine Mansfield* (Brighton: Harvester Press, 1986).

Gathorne-Hardy, Robert (ed.), *Ottoline, The Early Memoirs of Lady Ottoline Morrell* (London: Faber, 1963).

Gathorne-Hardy, Robert (ed.), *Ottoline at Garsington, Memoirs of Lady Ottoline Morrell 1915–1918* (London: Faber, 1974).

Gerhardie, William, *Memoirs of a Polyglot* (London: Macdonald, 1931).

Gerzina, Gretchen, *Carrington, a Life of Dora Carrington 1893–1932* (London: John Murray, 1989).

Glenavy, Lady Beatrice, *Today We Will Only Gossip* (London: Constable, 1964).

Gordon, Ian A., *Katherine Mansfield* (London: Longmans, Green & Co. for the British Council and National Book League, 1954).

Hankin, C.A. (ed.), *The Letters of John Middleton Murry to Katherine Mansfield* (London: Constable, 1983).

Hanson, Clare and Gurr, Andrew, *Katherine Mansfield* (Basingstoke: Macmillan, 1981).

Hassall, Christopher, *Edward Marsh, Patron of the Arts* (London: Longmans, 1959).

Hignett, Sean, *Brett* (London: Hodder and Stoughton, 1984).

Holroyd, Michael, *Lytton Strachey, Volume II, The Years of Achievement (1910–1932)* (London: Heinemann, 1968).

Hormasji, Nariman, *Katherine Mansfield, An Appraisal* (London: Collins, 1967).

Kaplan, Sydney Janet, *Katherine Mansfield and the Origins of Modernist Fiction* (Ithaca, New York: Cornell University Press, 1991).

Kaye, Elaine, *A History of Queen's College, London 1848–1972* (London: Chatto and Windus, 1972).

Kennedy, Julie, *Katherine Mansfield in Picton* (Auckland: Cape Catley, 2000).

Kynaston, David, *Archie's Last Stand* (London: Queen Anne Press, 1984).

Lawlor, P.A., *The Mystery of Maata* (Wellington: Beltane Book Bureau, 1946).

Lea, F.A., *The Life of John Middleton Murry* (London: Methuen, 1959).

Lee, Hermione, *Virginia Woolf* (London: Vintage, 1997).

Levy, Paul (ed.), *The Letters of Lytton Strachey* (London: Viking, 2005).

Lilley, George, *A Bibliography of John Middleton Murry 1889–1957* (London: Dawson, 1974).

L.M. [Ida Baker], *Katherine Mansfield, the Memories of LM* (London: Michael Joseph, 1971).

Mairet, Philip, *A.R. Orage, a Memoir* (New York: University Books, 1966).

Mansfield, Katherine, *Manuscripts in the Alexander Turnbull Library* (Wellington: National Library of New Zealand, 1988).

Mantz, Ruth Elvish, *The Critical Bibliography of Katherine Mansfield* (London: Constable, 1931).

Mantz, Ruth Elvish and Murry, J. Middleton, *The Life of Katherine Mansfield* (London: Constable, 1933).

Martin, Wallace, *The 'New Age' Under Orage* (Manchester: Manchester University Press, 1967).

Maurois, André, *Poets and Prophets* (London: Cassell, 1936).

Meyers, Jeffrey, *Married to Genius* (London: London Magazine Editions, 1977).

Meyers, Jeffrey, *Modigliani, A Life* (London: Duckworth, 2006).

Michel, Paulette and Dupuis, Michel (eds), *The Fine Instrument, Essays on Katherine Mansfield* (Sydney: Dangeroo Press, 1989).

Moore, James, *Gurdjieff, The Anatomy of a Myth* (Shaftesbury: Element, 1991).

Moore, James, *Gurdjieff and Mansfield* (London: Routledge and Kegan Paul, 1980).

Morris, Margaret, *The Art of J.D. Fergusson, A Biased Biography* (Glasgow: Blackie, 1974).

Murry, John Middleton, *Between Two Worlds, an Autobiography* (London: Jonathan Cape, 1935).

Murry, John Middleton, *Katherine Mansfield and Other Literary Portraits* (London: Peter Nevill, 1949).

Murry, John Middleton, *Katherine Mansfield and Other Literary Studies* (London: Constable, 1959).

Murry, Katherine Middleton, *Beloved Quixote, The Unknown Life of John Middleton Murry* (London: Souvenir Press, 1986).

Nehls, Edward (ed.), *D.H. Lawrence, A Composite Biography, Volume I* (Wisconsin: Madison, 1957).

Nicholson, Nigel (ed.), *The Question of Things Happening, the Letters of Virginia Woolf: Vol. II 1912–1922* (London: Hogarth Press, 1976).

Norburn, Roger, *A James Joyce Chronology* (Basingstoke: Palgrave Macmillan, 2004).

Orage, A.R., *Selected Essays and Critical Writings*, ed. Herbert Read and Denis Saurat (London: Stanley Nott, 1935).

O'Sullivan, Vincent, *Katherine Mansfield's New Zealand* (London: Frederick Mullen, 1975).

Ouspensky, P.D., *In Search of the Miraculous* (London: Routledge and Kegan Paul, 1950).

Pauwels, Louis, *Gurdjieff* (Douglas, Isle of Man: Times Press, 1964).

Peters, Fritz, *Gurdjieff* (London: Wildwood House, 1976).

Preston, Peter, *A D.H. Lawrence Chronology* (Basingstoke: Macmillan, 1994).

Ricketts, Harry, *Worlds of Katherine Mansfield* (Palmerston North, New Zealand: Nagare Press, 1992).

Robinson, Roger (ed.), *Katherine Mansfield, In from the Margin* (London: Louisiana State University Press, 1994).

Russell, Bertrand, *The Autobiography of Bertrand Russell Volume II 1914–1944* (London: Allen and Unwin, 1968).

Scott, Margaret, *Recollecting Mansfield* (Auckland: Random House, 2001).

Seymour, Miranda, *Ottoline Morrell, Life on the Grand Scale* (Sevenoaks: Hodder and Stoughton, 1992).

Shaw, Helen (ed.), *Dear Lady Ginger, an exchange of letters between Lady Ottoline Morrell and D'Arcy Cresswell* (London: Century, 1983).

Smith, Angela, *Katherine Mansfield, A Literary Life* (Basingstoke: Palgrave, 2000).

Smith, Angela, *Katherine Mansfield and Virginia Woolf, A Public of Two* (Oxford: Clarendon, 1999).

Smith, Grover (ed.), *Letters of Aldous Huxley* (London: Chatto and Windus, 1969).

Stone, Jean E., *Katherine Mansfield, Publications in Australia 1907–1909* (Sydney: Wentworth Books, 1977).

Swinnerton, Frank, *Figures in the Foreground* (London: Hutchinson, 1963).

Swinnerton, Frank, *A London Bookman* (London: Martin Secker, 1928).

Swinnerton, Frank, *Swinnerton, An Autobiography* (London: Hutchinson, 1937).

Tedlock, E.W. (ed.), *Frieda Lawrence, The Memoirs and Correspondence* (London: Heinemann, 1961).

Thomson, John Mansfield, *The Oxford History of New Zealand Music* (Auckland: Oxford University Press, 1991).

Usborne, Karen, *'Elizabeth', The Author of 'Elizabeth and Her German Garden'* (London: Bodley Head, 1986).

Willy, Margaret, *Three Women Diarists, Celia Fiennes, Dorothy Wordsworth, Katherine Mansfield* (London: Longmans, Green & Co. for the British Council and National Book League, 1964).

Woods, Joanna, *Katerina, The Russian World of Katherine Mansfield* (Harmondsworth: Penguin, 2001).

Woolf, Leonard, *Beginning Again, An autobiography of the years 1911–1918* (London: Hogarth Press, 1964).

Woolf, Leonard (ed.), *A Writer's Diary, Being Extracts from the diary of Virginia Woolf* (London: Hogarth Press, 1953).

Worthen, John, *D.H. Lawrence, The Life of an Outsider* (London: Allen Lane, 2005).

D.

Arkell, David, 'The Tigers' Lair in Gray's Inn Road' (in *Camden History Review*, Nov. 1980).

Clarke, Brice, 'Katherine Mansfield's Illness' (in *Proceedings of the Royal Society of Medicine*, Vol. 48, April 1955).

Coles, Gladys Mary, 'Katherine Mansfield and William Gerhardie' (in *Contemporary Review*, July 1976).

Conroy, Geraldine L., '"Our Perhaps Uncommon Friendship": The Relationship Between S.S. Koteliansky and Katherine Mansfield' (in *Modern Fiction Studies*, 24, No. 3, 1978).

Dudding, Robin (ed.), *Landfall* (Christchurch) Vol. 26, No. 1, March 1972 contains 'Brave Love' by Katherine Mansfield transcribed and with a note by Margaret Scott.

Gordon, Ian A., 'The Editing of Katherine Mansfield's Journal and Scrapbook' (in *Landfall* (Christchurch) Vol. 13, No. 1, March 1959).

Grindea, Miron (ed.), *ADAM International Review* No. 300, 1963–1965 contains letters by KM, an editorial partly on her and other material.

Grindea, Miron (ed.), *ADAM International Review* Nos. 370–375, 1972–1973. A special number devoted to KM.

Hudson, Stephen, 'First Meetings with Katherine Mansfield' (in *Cornhill*, Autumn 1958).

Kafian, Adèle, 'The Last Days of Katherine Mansfield' (in *Adelphi* 23, Oct.–Dec. 1946).

Meyers, Jeffrey, 'Katherine Mansfield's "To Stanislaw Wyspiansky"' (in *Modern Fiction Studies*, Vol. 23, No. 4, Autumn 1978).

Meyers, Jeffrey, 'The Quest for Katherine Mansfield' (in *Biography*, Summer 1978).

Murry, John Middleton, 'A Friend in Need to Katherine Mansfield' (in *Adelphi* 24, July 1948).

Murry, John Middleton, 'Katherine Mansfield in France' (in *Atlantic Monthly*, Sept. 1949).

Olgivanna (Mrs Frank Lloyd Wright), 'The Last Days of Katherine Mansfield' (in *Bookman*, New York, 73, March 1931).

Stone, Jean E., 'Katherine Mansfield [:] Australian Family Associations' (in *Biblionews* (Sydney) Third Series, Vol. 3, No. 4, 1978).

Sutherland, Ronald, 'Katherine Mansfield: Plagiarist, Disciple, or Ardent Admirer?' (in *Critique* 5, Fall 1962).

Waldron, Philip, 'Katherine Mansfield's *Journal*' (in *Twentieth Century Literature*, Jan. 1974).

E.

Aiken, Conrad, 'Your Obituary Well Written' in *Costumes by Eros* (1929).

Carco, Francis, *Les Innocents* (1916).

Downes, Cathy, *The Case of Katherine Mansfield* (Wellington: The Women's Play Press, 1995).

Huxley, Aldous, *Point Counter Point* (1928).

Huxley, Aldous, *Those Barren Leaves* (1925).

Isherwood, Christopher, *The World in the Evening* (1954).

Keefer, Janice Kulyk, *Thieves* (2003).

Lawrence, D.H., 'The Fox' in *The Ladybird* (1923).

Lawrence, D.H., 'Mother and Daughter', first published in the *New Criterion* (1929).

Lawrence, D.H., 'Smile' in *The Woman who Rode Away and Other Stories* (1928).

Lawrence, D.H., *Touch and Go,* a play in three acts (1920).

Lawrence, D.H., *Women in Love* (1921).

Orton, William, *The Last Romantic* (1937).

Stead, C.K., *Mansfield* (2004).

Tomalin, Claire, *The Winter Wife,* a play (1991).

Index

This index is divided into three main sections:

1. The publications of Katherine Mansfield:
   (a) the short stories of the five collections
   (b) the poems of *Poems of Katherine Mansfield* (ed. O'Sullivan)
   (c) other works
   (d) newspapers/periodicals which published Katherine Mansfield
2. People
3. Places:
   (a) New Zealand and Australia
   (b) The British Isles
   (c) Europe (and beyond)

1. The Publications of Katherine Mansfield

(a) the short stories of the five collections

'At Lehmann's' (*IGP*), 19
'At the Bay' (*GPOS*), 11, 76–8, 81, 83, 96, 102

'Bains Turcs' (*SCOS*), 27
'Bank Holiday' (*GPOS*), 68
'The Baron' (*IGP*), 18
'A Birthday' (*IGP*), 20
'The Black Cap' (*SCOS*), 42, 71
'Bliss' (*BOS*), 48, 52–4, 109
Bliss and Other Stories, 54, 69, 71–3, 78, 84

'The Canary' (*DNOS*), 86, 100
'Carnation' (*SCOS*), 51, 53
'The Child-Who-Was-Tired' (*IGP*), 18, 124
'A Cup of Tea' (*DNOS*), 81–2, 85

'Daphne' (*DNOS*), 79
'The Daughters of the Late Colonel' (*GPOS*), 70–1, 75–6, 79, 83–4, 105, 124

'A Dill Pickle' (*BOS*), 44
'The Doll's House' (*DNOS*), 3, 78–9, 81–2
'The Doves' Nest' (*DNOS*), 81, 86
The Doves' Nest and Other Stories, 76, 114

'The Escape' (*BOS*), 67

'Feuille d'Album' (*BOS*), 44
'The Fly' (*DNOS*), 83–4, 86, 97

'The Garden Party' (*GPOS*), 2, 8, 78, 82–3
The Garden Party and Other Stories, 78, 83–5, 122
'Germans at Meat' (*IGP*), 18

'Her First Ball' (*GPOS*), 76, 79
'Honesty' (*DNOS*), 78
'Honeymoon' (*DNOS*), 85
'How Pearl Button was Kidnapped' (*SCOS*), 10, 24

'An Ideal Family' (*GPOS*), 76–7
In a German Pension, 16–17, 21, 24, 64–5, 115, 122, 124
'An Indiscreet Journey' (*SCOS*), 33, 102

'Je ne parle pas français' (*BOS*),
   47–8, 54, 60, 64–6, 83, 102,
   117
'The Journey to Bruges' (*SCOS*), 21

'The Lady's Maid' (*GPOS*), 71–2
'Late at Night' (*SCOS*), 42
'Life of Ma Parker' (*GPOS*), 73
'The Little Girl' (*SCOS*), 24
'The Little Governess' (*BOS*), 33,
   35
'The Luft Bad' (*IGP*), 18

'The Man Without a Temperament'
   (*BOS*), 63–4
'Marriage à la Mode' (*GPOS*), 76, 80,
   109
'A Married Man's Story' (*DNOS*), 77
'Millie' (*SCOS*), 27
'Miss Brill' (*GPOS*), 70, 72–3
'Mr and Mrs Dove' (*GPOS*), 76
'Mr Reginald Peacock's Day' (*BOS*),
   42

'New Dresses' (*SCOS*), 24

'Pension Séguin' (*SCOS*), 26
'Pictures' (*BOS*), 42
'Poison' (*SCOS*), 70
'Prelude' (*BOS*), xvi, 2, 33, 43–5, 48,
   51–2, 64, 71, 77, 83, 96, 102,
   104, 114, 121, 129
'Psychology' (*BOS*), 121

'Revelations' (*BOS*), 66–7

'Second Violin' (*DNOS*), 77
'See-Saw' (*SCOS*), 58
'The Singing Lesson' (*GPOS*), 69,
   74
'The Sister of the Baroness' (*IGP*), 19
'Sixpence' (*SCOS*), 76, 79
'Six Years After' (*DNOS*), 78–9, 97
'Something Childish But Very
   Natural' (*SCOS*), 28, 120
Something Childish and Other Stories,
   12, 114

'Spring Pictures' (*SCOS*), 33
'The Stranger' (*GPOS*), 16, 70, 72
'A Suburban Fairy' (*SCOS*), 56
'Such a Sweet Old Lady' (*DNOS*),
   76
'Sun and Moon' (*BOS*), 47, 69
'Susannah' (*DNOS*), 76

'Taking the Veil' (*DNOS*), 82–3
'This Flower' (*SCOS*), 63
'The Tiredness of Rosabel' (*SCOS*),
   12
'A Truthful Adventure' (*SCOS*), 21
'Two Tuppenny Ones, Please'
   (*SCOS*), 42

'Violet' (*SCOS*), 26
'The Voyage' (*GPOS*), 76–7, 80,
   84

'Weak Heart' (*DNOS*), 78–9
'Widowed' (*DNOS*), 78
'The Wind Blows' (*BOS*), 34, 68
'The Woman at the Store' (*SCOS*),
   10–11, 22, 64
'The Wrong House' (*SCOS*), 63

'The Young Girl' (*GPOS*), 69–70

**(b) the poems of *Poems
of Katherine Mansfield*
(ed. O'Sullivan)**

'Along the Gray's Inn Road', 21
'Arrival', 51
'The Awakening River', 22

'The Butterfly', 51

'Countrywomen', 28
'Covering Wings', 56

'Dame Seule', 51
'Deaf House Agent', 30

'The Earth-Child in the Grass', 24
'Et Après', 61

'Fairy Tale', 56
'Firelight', 56
'Floryan nachdenklich', 26

'He wrote', 61

'In the Botanical Gardens', 11
'In the Rangitaiki Valley', 10

'Jangling Memory', 25

'Leves Amores', 11
'A Little Girl's Prayer', 58
'Loneliness', 18

'Malade', 51
'The Meeting', 29

'The New Husband', 61
'Night Scented Stock', 43
'November', 13, 17

'October' – *see* 'November'
'Old-Fashioned Widow's Song',
    63
'The Opal Dream Cave', 18, 25

'Pic-Nic', 51

'Revelation', 14

'Sea', 18, 25
'The Sea Child', 18
'Sea Song', 26
'Secret Flowers', 59
'Silhouettes', 9
'Sorrowing Love', 57
'Stars', 28
'Strawberries and the Sailing
    Ship', 51
'The Students' Room', 5
'Sunset', 63

'There Was a Child Once', 26,
    120
'To God the Father', 25
'To L.H.B. (1894–1915)', 37, 97

'To Stanislaw Wyspiansky', 16, 19,
    124
'The Trio', 14

'Very Early Spring', 22
'Vignette – By the Sea', 12
'Vignette – I look out through the
    window', 14
'Vignettes', 9, 24
'Vignette – Summer in Winter', 9
'Vignette – Through the Autumn
    afternoon', 8

'Why Love is Blind', 13
'The Winter Fire', 14
'The Wounded Bird', 86

(c) other works

'About Pat' (story), 5
'An Album Leaf' (story), 44
'The Aloe' (story), xvi, 33, 37–8, 43,
    114
'The Apple Tree' (story), 34

'Brave Love' (story), 32

'A Day in Bed' (poem), 17

'The Education of Audrey' (sketch),
    11, 15
'E. M. Forster' (fragment), 41
'Enna Blake' (story), 2

'A Fairy Story' (story), 19
'The Festival of the Coronation
    (with apologies to Theocritus)'
    (pastiche), 20

'Geneva' (fragment), 40–1
'Green Goggles' (parody), 24

'A Happy Christmas Eve' (story), 3
'His Sister's Keeper' (story), 15
'The House' (story), 25

'In a Café' (story), 11
'In Confidence' (sketch), 42

140 *Index*

Juliet (abandoned novel), 6

'The Laurels' (playlet), 40, 103, 125
'Living Alone' (fragment), 41
'The Lost Battle' – *see* 'Geneva'

Maata (abandoned novel), 27–8
'A Marriage of Passion' (satire), 22

'The New Baby' (fragmentary story), 83

'Old Tar' (story), 27–8

'Perambulations' (sketch), 56
'A Pic-Nic' (dialogue/film script), 42
'The Picture' (story), 42, 59, 123

'A Ship in the Harbour' – *see* Toots'
'Stay-laces' (dialogue), 35

'Toots' (play), 41–2
'Travelling Alone' – *see* 'Geneva'
'Two Songs: Love's Entreaty' and 'Night' (words for songs), 4

'Youth' (poem), 11

(d) newspapers/periodicals which published Katherine Mansfield

Adelphi, 110, 114–15
Art and Letters, 42, 59, 66, 123
Athenaeum, 21, 55–73, 79, 98–9, 102, 109, 111–12, 114–15, 119–20, 125–6, 128–9

Blue Review, 26–7, 101, 128

Daily News, 17, 72, 79–80
Dominion (New Zealand), 12, 26

English Review, 52–3
Evening Post (New Zealand), 15, 31

Gazeta Poniedzialkowa (Poland), 19

Hearth and Home, 25
The High School Reporter (New Zealand), 2–3

Idler, 18

London Mercury, 72, 75, 81
Lone Hand (Australia), 17

Nation, 52–3, 58, 67
Nation & the Athenaeum, 73, 76, 82, 84–5, 87
Native Companion (Australia), 9, 11, 24, 95
New Age, 18–25, 41–2, 44–5, 88, 108, 118–19
New Zealand Free Lance, 8, 13
New Zealand Times, 28

Open Window, 19

Pall Mall Magazine, 18

Queen's College Magazine, 4–5

Rhythm, 20, 22–6, 101–4, 106, 108, 111–12, 114, 120, 122–3, 126

Saturday Westminster Gazette, 26–7, 82–3
Signature, 34–6
Sketch, 83
Sphere, 74, 76–7, 79–80, 84–5
Story-teller, 85

Times Literary Supplement (TLS), 28, 50–1, 64
T. P.'s Weekly, 25
Triad (New Zealand), 13

Weekly Westminster Gazette, 83
Westminster Gazette, 24, 27, 82

2. People

(Note: A number in **bold** indicates an entry in the 'Who's Who' section.)

Aiken, Conrad, 75, 78
Ainger, Dr, 45, 49
Alpers, Antony, 94, 100, 119
Ansaldi, Dr, 60–1
Asquith, H. H., 98
'Aunt Belle': *see* Dyer, Belle
Austen, Jane, 80
Austin, Alfred, 20

Baker, Ida Constance, xvi, xvii, 4–5,
    8–9, 13, 15–21, 29, 39, 41,
    46–53, 59–63, 68–70, 73–7, 80,
    82, 84–91, **93–4**, 99, 120–1,
    127–8
Banks, George, 26, 104
Bannatyne and Co., W. M., 1, 95
Barrie, J. M., 40, 102
Bartrick-Baker, Vere, 125
Beauchamp, Annie, 1–4, 6, 8, 10,
    13, 15–17, 22, 29, 37, 47, 50,
    53, **94–5**, 96–7
Beauchamp, Arthur, 18, 95, 128
Beauchamp, Charlotte ('Chaddie'),
    xvi, 1–4, 6, 10, 12, 28, 37, 45–6,
    53, 68, 77, 87–8, 90–1, 113
Beauchamp, Connie, 61, 64–5, 70
Beauchamp, Gwendoline, 1–2
Beauchamp, Harold, xvii, 1–4, 6,
    8–9, 12–13, 16, 31, 37, 45, 54,
    59–61, 63, 65, 75, 79, 81, 84–8,
    91, 94, **95–6**, 97, 116, 127
Beauchamp, Henry Herron, 4–5, 7,
    96–7, 128
Beauchamp, Jeanne, 1–4, 14, 17, 27,
    77–8, 82, 87, 89–91, 96
Beauchamp, John, 96
Beauchamp, Leslie Heron, xvi, 1–4,
    32, 34–5, 58, **96–7**, 106, 117
Beauchamp, Mary Annette
    ('Elizabeth'), 2, 4, 56, 76–8,
    80–4, 86, 91, 94, 96, **97–8**, 121
Beauchamp, Mary Elizabeth, 45, 95
Beauchamp, Sydney, 54

Beauchamp, Vera, 1–4, 6, 11, 13–14,
    82, 84
Bell, Clive, 57, 128
Bell, Vanessa, 41–3, 54, 128
Belloc, Hilaire, 98, 118
Belloc-Lowndes, Marie, xvii, 75, **98**,
    112
Bendall, Edith, 8, 11–12
Bennett, Arnold, 11, 18, 20, 69, 91,
    118, 126
Berkman, Sylvia, 94
Bibesco, Elizabeth, 71–2, 74, **98**, 116
Bieler, Mme., 21
Bishop, Henry, 19–20
Bloy, Léon, 43
Bouchage, Dr, 69, 71, 74–5
Bowden, George, xvii, 15–16, 18, 23,
    44, **99–100**
Boyd, Mrs Charley, 14
Brady, E. J., 9
Brechenmacher family, 17
Brett, Dorothy, xvii, 35, 39–40,
    44–5, 50, 53, 55, 57–8, 68–9,
    74–81, 83–8, 90–1, **100**, 103–4,
    115–17
Bright, Laura Kate, 30–1, 63, 96
Brontë, Emily, 58
Brooke, Rupert, 24, 31, 112
Bunin, Ivan, 85

Campbell, Beatrice, 25, 27, 38, 55,
    100, **101**
Campbell, Gordon, 27, 31–2, 38, 55,
    100, **101**
Cannan, Gilbert, 24–6, 31, 57, 60,
    101–2, 106, 110
Cannan, Mary, 25–6, 31, 73
Carco, Francis, 23, 31–4, **102**,
    117
Carrington, Dora, 39–40, **103**, 106,
    125
Cézanne, Paul, 5, 77
Chaucer, Geoffrey, 75

Chekhov, Anton, 4, 52, 56–60, 62–3, 65, 67, 69, 71–2, 79, 85–6, 105, 110, 124
Chesterton, G. K., 20, 118
Cobden-Sanderson, Richard, 79, 105, 117
Colette, 31, 62
Conrad, Joseph, 7, 20, 40, 58, 67, 91
Crippen, Dr, 17, 19

Daudet, Alphonse, 44
De la Mare, Walter, 18, 22, 72–3, **103**
Dickens, Charles, 36
Donat, Dr, 82
Dostoevsky, Fyodor, 32, 50, 60–1, 89, 110, 115, 126
Drey, Anne Estelle, 25, 32, 46, 50–3, 65, 67, 80–1, **103–4**, 124–5
Drey, O. Raymond, 25, 72, 104
Dyer, Belle ('Aunt Belle'), 1–4, 6–7, 14, 45, 53, 94
Dyer, Joseph, 94
Dyer, Margaret, Isabella ('Granny Dyer'), 1–2, 7, 82, 94–5

Ebbetts family, 10
Eliot, T. S., 40, 42–3, 55, 57–8, 62, 66–7, 74, 81, 90, 112, 123

Fairbanks, Douglas, 67
Fergusson, J.D., 23, 44–5, 47, 50–1, **104**
Forster, E. M., 7, 11, 18, 41, 68, 90, 97, 99, 129
Foster, Dr, 62
France, Anatole, 72, 80
French, Vera, 17
Fry, Roger, 43, 57–8
Fullerton, Jinnie, 61, 64–5, 70

Galsworthy, John, 5, 23, 71, 79, 124
Garnett, Constance, 61, 72
Garnett, Edward, 26, 88
Gaudier-Brzeska, Henri, 23–6, 34, **104–5**

Gerhardie, William, 76, 78–9, 83–7, **105**
Gertler, Mark, 31, 38, 55, 58, 100, 103, **105–6**, 110, 112
Gibson, Wilfrid, 21
Goethe, Johann Wolfgang von, 85
Goodyear, Frederick, 28, 37–8, 41–2, **106–7**
Gorki, Maxim, 54, 87, 110
Gozzano, Guido, 61
Grace, Martha: *see* Mahupuku, Maata
Granville, Charles ('Stephen Swift'), 21, 23–4, 112
Graves, Robert, 43
Gurdjieff, George Ivanovich, 88–90, 94, **107–8**, 112, 119–21

Hamsun, Knut, 62, 67
Hardy, Thomas, 15, 28, 51, 66, 79, 81, 90
Harris, Frank, 23, 25
Hastings, Beatrice, 19–22, 25, 33, **108**, 119
Heinemann, Francis, 19
Hill, Mr, 10
Honey, Mrs, 52
Hope, Anthony, 4
Housman, Laurence, 21
Hudson, Stephen: *see* Schiff, Sydney
Hutchinson, Mary, 39, 43
Hutchinson, St John, 39–40, 57
Huxley, Aldous, 40, 42–3, 45, 55, 72, 91, **109**, 114, 123, 126
Huxley, Julian, 42, 109

James, Henry, 36, 66, 113
Joyce, James, 28, 36, 58, 80–1, 84–5, 123

Keynes, J. M., 39, 128
Koteliansky, Samuel Solomonovitch, 31–3, 35, 38–9, 53, 55–60, 62–5, 73, 78–80, 87, 89, 94, **109–11**

Lawrence, D. H., 20, 22, 25–8, 30–4,
    36–40, 53–6, 64, 71–3, 76–7,
    80–1, 87–91, 100, 105–6, 110,
    111–12, 113–16, 121, 126
Lawrence, Frieda, 27, 30–3, 36,
    38–9, 56, 100, 111, **112**
Leblanc, Georges, 74
Leithead, Ann, 10
Lenin, Vladimir Ilyich, 84
Lewis, Wyndham, 46, 85, 88, 123
L. M.: *see* Baker, Ida Constance
Locke-Ellis, Vivian, 88
Lynd, Sylvia, 72, 77–8

Macaulay, Rose, 56, 67
MacCarthy, Desmond, 72
Mackenzie, Compton, 60, 66–7
Mahupuku, Maata, 3, 8
Mander, Jane, 67
Manoukhin, Dr, 78–80, 82, 85,
    88–9, 111
Mantz, Ruth Elvish, 115
Marlowe, Christopher, 75
Marsh, Edward, 23–5, 98, 106,
    112–13
Maugham, Somerset, 31, 57
Maupassant, Guy de, 71
Meredith, George, 15, 54
Mills, Tom, 24, 95
Miss Swainson's school, 3
Modigliani, Amedeo, 62, 108
Moody-Manners Opera Company:
    see Trowell, Garnett
Moore, Thomas, 4
Morrell, Ottoline, xvii, 32, 38, 40–3,
    45–50, 52–4, 57–9, 63, 73–6, 80,
    100, 106, 109–10, **113–14**
Morrell, Philip, 49, 113
Murry, John Middleton, xvi, xvii, 1,
    22–78, 80, 82–91, 94–113,
    114–17, 118–24, 126, 128
Murry, Richard, xvii, 43–4, 60, 65,
    67, 72, 75, 77, 84–5, 114, **117**

Nathan, Walter, 2
Nesbit, E., 5, 21
Neuberg, Victor, 22–3

Newland-Pedley, F., 36, **117–18**
Nitsch, Rosa, 16
Nys, Maria, 40

Orage, A. R., 18–19, 22–3, 33, 73,
    87–9, 99, 107–8, **118–19**,
    120
Orton, William, 19, 21, **119–20**
Ouspensky, P. D., 88, 107, 119,
    120–1

Parker, Millie, 9–10
Payne, Sylvia, 4–7, 12
Pickford, Mary, 67
Pinker, Eric, 83
Pinker, J. B., 21, 70, 77–9, 82–3,
    113
Poe, Edgar Allan, 4–5
Pound, Ezra, 15, 36, 55, 67, 80, 90,
    118
Proust, Marcel, 25, 80–1, 123
Putnam, Martha, 8, 11

Renshaw, Charles, 96
Rice, Anne Estelle: *see* Drey, Anne
    Estelle
Richards, Grant, 64, 122
Rippmann, Walter, 4
Robins, Elizabeth, 12, 67
Rosenberg, Isaac, 105–6
Ross, Robert, 43, 54
Rouse, Gwen, 128
Ruddick, Marion, 2–3
Russell, Bertrand, 34, 40–1, 57, 109,
    121–2

Sadleir, Michael, 20, 66, 73, 78–9,
    114, **122**
Saleeby, Dr C. W., 15
Santayana, George, 80, 113
Sassoon, Siegfried, 40, 42, 52
Schiff, Sydney, 60, 65–7, 69, 71,
    80–1, 84–5, 88, **122–3**
Schiff, Violet, 66, 68, 78, 84–5, 87–8,
    123
Scholefield, Guy, 96
Seddon, Tom, 10

Shakespeare, William, 37, 48, 66, 75
Shaw, G. B., 5, 22, 55, 60, 72, 118,
    124
Sheehan, Patrick, 5
Shorter, Clement, 84–5
Sobieniowski, Floryan, 16–17, 19,
    24, 26, 33, 68–9, **123–4**
Sorapure, Victor, 53, 55, 58–9, 61,
    71–2, 75, 87–8, 121, **124–5**
Spahlinger, Dr, 74
Squire, J. C., 73
Stein, Gertrude, 15, 69
Stendhal, 33
Stephani, Dr, 75
Strachey, Lytton, 35, 39–40, 46,
    58–9, 72, 103, 106, **125**, 129
Strindberg, August, 22, 24
Sullivan, J. W. N., 55, 65, 109,
    125–6
Swift, Stephen: *see* Granville,
    Charles
Swinnerton, Frank, 24, 57, 60,
    126
Synge, J. M., 7, 15, 24

Tchehov, Anton: *see* Chekhov,
    Anton
Theocritus, 20, 28
Thomas, Edward, 40, 109
Tolstoy, Leo, 18, 60, 68–9, 75, 89,
    110
Tomlinson, H. M., 56
Trinder, W. Harry, 7, 14
Trowell family, 9, 13–15, 127
Trowell, Garnett, xvii, 3–4, 6, 9,
    13–15, 19, 99, **127**
Trowell, Thomas, 3–6, 8–9, 11–13,
    127–8
Turgenev, Ivan, 30
Tynan, Katherine, 21

Van Gogh, Vincent, 11, 80

Wallace, Dr Lewis, 81
Walpole, Hugh, 59, 69, 97
Walter, Charlie, 17
Ward, Eileen, 13

Waterlow, Sydney, 40, 73–4, **129**
Webber, Mr and Mrs, 10
Webster, Dr, 87
Weekley, Frieda: *see* Lawrence,
    Frieda
Wells, H. G., 11, 15, 18, 20, 24, 71,
    118, 126
Wharton, Edith, 20, 62, 71
Whitman, Walt, 42
Wilde, Oscar, 4, 9, 123
Wishart, Margaret, 13–14, 99
Wood, Clara, 6
Woolf, Leonard, 40–1, 43–4, 50–2,
    56, 58, 61, 79, 104, 110,
    129
Woolf, Virginia, xvii, 31, 39–45,
    50–8, 60–1, 67, 72–3, 78, 81, 84,
    100, 104, 110, **128–9**
Wordsworth, Dorothy, 50
Wordsworth, William, 48

Yeats, W. B., 28, 40, 48, 91,
    113
Young, Dr, 89

3. Places

(a) New Zealand and Australia

Anakiwa, 2
Ararat, 95
Atiamuri, 10

Eskdale, 10–11

Galatea, 10

Hastings, 10–11
Hobart, 16
Huka Falls, 11

Karori, 2, 5, 27

Lake Taupo, 11
Lyttleton, 13

Melbourne, 9, 95

Napier, 10–11

Picton, 2, 18, 45, 95

Rangitaiki, 10–11
Rotorua, 10
Ruatahuna, 10
Rununga, 11

Sydney, 11, 94, 97

Tarawera, 10–11
Te Pohue, 10–11
Te Whaiti, 10

Umuroa, 10
Urewera, 10

Waikato River, 11
Waiotapu, 10
Waipunga Falls and River, 10
Wanganui, 95
Wellington, 1–3, 7, 9–13, 17, 52, 88,
    95–6, 111

(b) The British Isles

Asheham (Sussex), 43–4, 53

Bexley (Kent), 4–5
Birmingham, 13
Bloomsbury, 32, 35, 39, 113,
    128–9
Broadstairs (Kent), 27

Chesham (Bucks), 30
Cholesbury (Bucks), 26, 101
Cornwall, 30, 36, 51
Crawley (Sussex), 22

Devonport (Devon), 14
Ditchling-on-Sea (Sussex), 20
Dublin, 27, 101

Eastbourne (Sussex), 5

Garsington (Oxon), 38–46, 52, 56,
    58, 109, 113, 117, 121, 125
Glasgow, 15
Great Missenden (Bucks), 31

Higher Tregerthen (Cornwall), 38, 111
Howth, 27, 101

Liverpool, 15
London: passim
Looe (Cornwall), 50–1, 104

Malvern (Worcestershire), 4
Mylor (Cornwall), 38–9, 106

Oxford, 22–3, 29, 75, 105–6, 114

Pulborough (Sussex), 30, 33

Rottingdean (Sussex), 18, 23, 25
Runcton (Sussex), 24–5, 104, 124

Selsfield (Sussex), 88
Sheffield, 4
Stratford-on-Avon, 66

Tadworth (Surrey), 53

Udimore (Sussex), 30
Upper Warlingham (Surrey), 14

West Wittering (Sussex), 39

Zennor (Cornwall), 37–8

(c) Europe (and beyond)

Armentières, 35
Arras, 42, 106
Avon, 88–9, 91, 96, 107, 116–17,
    119, 121

Bad Wörishofen, 16
Bandol, 35–7, 46–9, 104, 111,
    118
Bruges, 21, 120
Brussels, 6, 16

Caen, 94
Canary Islands, 3
Cassis, 35

Fontainebleau, 88–9, 91, 107
Frankfurt, 4

Geneva, 21–2, 108, 120
Gray, 32–3, 102

Lisieux, 94

Marseilles, 35, 37, 47, 49
Menton, 61, 63, 65–6, 68, 72, 74–5,
    99, 123
Monaco, 66
Montana, 76, 97–8
Monte Carlo, 65
Montevideo, 13–14
Montreux, 75

Nice, 66

Ospedaletti, 59–63

Paris, 6, 14, 23, 25, 28–9, 33,
    46–7, 49, 66, 68–9, 80,
    82–5, 88–9, 102–4, 106,
    108

Randogne, 76, 85–6, 97
Rhodesia, 20–1, 29, 39, 94
Roquebrune, 123

San Remo, 58–60
Sierre, 75, 82, 86–7, 105, 120
Stuttgart, 16

Tenerife, 13

Versailles, 14